SICILIAN MILLIONAIRE, BOUGHT BRIDE

BY
CATHERINE SPENCER

MILLS & BOON®
Pure reading pleasure™

First published in Great Britain 2008
Harlequin Mills & Boon Limited,
Eton House, 18-24 Paradise Road, Richmond, Surrey TW9 1SR

© Spencer Books Limited 2008

ISBN: 978 0 263 86469 4

Set in Times Roman 10½ on 12¾ pt
01-1008-47802

Printed and bound in Spain
by Litografia Rosés, S.A., Barcelona

SICILIAN MILLIONAIRE, BOUGHT BRIDE

CHAPTER ONE

TERSE AND ENIGMATIC, the letter sat on Corinne Mallory's dressing table, held in place by a can of hair spray. Hardly a fitting resting place, she supposed, for correspondence written on vellum embossed with an ornate gold family crest. On the other hand, considering her initial response had been to decline its autocratic summons, it was a miracle that she hadn't tossed the whole works in the garbage.

But the name at the end of the typed missive, signed in bold, impatient script, had given her pause. Raffaello Orsini had been married to her dearest friend, and Lindsay had been crazy about him, right up to the day she died. That alone had made Corinne swallow her pride and accede to his wishes. Whatever the reason for his sudden visit to Canada, loyalty to Lindsay's memory demanded Corinne not refuse him.

Now that she was just two short hours away from meeting the man face-to-face for the first time, however, she wasn't so sure she'd made the right decision. What did one wear to an invitation that smacked more of a command performance than a request?

Eyeing the limited contents of her closet, she decided

basic black was probably the most appropriate choice. With pearls. Dinner at the Pan Pacific, Vancouver's most prestigious hotel, called for a touch of elegance, even if the pearls in question weren't the real thing, and the black dress made of faux silk.

At least her black pumps came with a designer emblem on the instep, a reminder of the time when she'd been able to afford a few luxuries.

A reminder, too, of Lindsay, a tiny woman full of big dreams, who hadn't believed in the word "can't."

We'll buy some run-down, flea-bitten old place in the right part of town, and turn it into a boutique hotel, Corinne. I'll take care of housekeeping and decor, and you'll be in charge of the kitchen.

We'll need a fairy godmother to accomplish that.

Not us! We can do anything we set our minds to. Nothing's going to derail us.

What if we fall in love and get married?

It'll have to be to men who share our vision. She'd flashed her dimpled smile. *And it'd help if they were also very, very rich!*

And if they're not?

It won't matter, because we'll make our own luck. We can do this, Corinne. I know we can. We'll call it The Bowman-Raines Hotel, and have a great big old BR emblazoned over the front entrance. By the time we're thirty, we'll be famous for our hospitality and our dining room. People will kill to stay with us....

But all that was before Lindsay went to Sicily on holiday, and fell in love with Raffaello Orsini who was indeed very, very rich, but who had no interest whatsoever in sharing her dreams. Instead he'd converted her to his. Forgetting all about creating the most acclaimed hotel in the Pacific northwest, she'd moved halfway around the world to be his wife and start a family.

And the luck she'd believed in so fiercely? It had turned on her, striking her down at twenty-four with leukemia, and leaving her three-year-old daughter motherless.

Swamped in memories, Corinne blinked back the incipient tears, leaned closer to the mirror to sweep a mascara wand over her lashes and tried to remember the last time she'd worn eye makeup. Far too long ago, judging by the finished effect, but it would have to do, and really, what did it matter? Whatever the reason for his sudden visit, Raffaello Orsini certainly hadn't been inspired by a burning desire to evaluate her artistry with cosmetics.

Downstairs, she heard Mrs. Lehman, her next-door neighbor and baby-sitter, rattling dishes as she served Matthew his supper.

Matthew hadn't been happy that his mother was going out. "I hate it when you go to work," he'd announced, his lower lip trembling ominously.

With good reason, Corinne had to admit. She frequently missed tucking her son into bed, because her work too often involved late nights and time during his school holidays. It was the nature of the beast and much though she'd have preferred it otherwise, there wasn't much she could do about it, not if she wanted to keep a roof over their heads and food on the table.

"I won't be late, and I'll make blueberry pancakes for breakfast," she promised. "Be a good boy for Mrs. Lehman, and don't give her a hard time about going to bed, okay?"

"I might," he warned balefully. Although only four, he'd recently developed an alarming talent for blackmail. He was becoming, in fact, quite a handful. But Corinne hoped tonight wouldn't be one of those nights when she arrived home to find Mrs. Lehman exhausted from fighting to get him to bed, and Matthew still racing up and down the stairs every fifteen minutes and generally raising mayhem.

I should be staying home, Corinne thought, the familiar guilt sweeping over her as smoothly as the black dress slid past her hips. But the letter pulled at her, and even though she could have recited it word for word from memory, she picked it up and scoured it yet again, as if the writer's reason for sending it might be hidden between the lines.

Villa di Cascata
Sicily
January 6, 2008
Signora Mallory:
I shall be in Vancouver later this month on a matter of some urgency recently brought to my attention and which I wish to discuss with you in confidence.

I have reservations at the Pan Pacific Hotel and would appreciate your joining me there for dinner on Friday, January 28, a date I trust you find convenient. Unless I hear otherwise, I shall send a car for you at seven-thirty.
Kindest regards,
Raffaello Orsini

But just as with the first reading, there was nothing. No hint of what she might expect. And if the racket taking place in the kitchen was anything to go by, Matthew was gearing up to give poor Mrs. Lehman another night of grief.

"This had better be good, Mr. Orsini," Corinne muttered, tossing the letter aside, and taking a last glance in the mirror before going downstairs to appease a little boy who had no memory of his father, and whose mother seemed to be making a lousy job of doing double duty as a parent.

The view, Raffaello decided, was impressive. To the north, snowcapped mountains glimmered in carved splendor against the clear night sky. The lights of a bridge spanning the entrance to the harbor looped like so many diamonds above the Narrows. And closer at hand, almost directly below his suite, a yacht some twenty-five meters long or more rocked gently at its moorage.

Not Sicily, by any stretch of the imagination, but arresting nonetheless, as much because it had been Lindsay's home, a setting both wild and sophisticated, beautiful and intriguing, just like her.

Two years ago, one year even, and he could not have come here. The pain had been too raw, his grief too filled with anger. But time had a way of healing even the most savage wounds; of gilding the memories that were his wife's legacy, and turning them into a source of comfort. "I do this for you, *amore mio,*" he murmured, raising his eyes to the heavens.

Somewhere in the city below, a church bell rang out, eight solemn chimes. The woman, Corinne Mallory, was late. Impatient to get down to the business of the evening and be done with it, he paced to the telephone and buzzed the front desk to remind whoever was in charge that she should be directed to his suite when—*if*—she showed up. What he had to propose was not something to be aired in public.

Another ten minutes dragged past before she arrived, her knock so sudden and peremptory that his hackles rose. Curbing his irritation, he shot his cuffs and tugged his lapels into place.

Remember she was Lindsay's best friend. That does not mean she has to be yours, but it will be better for everyone if you can at least establish a sympathetic cordiality, he cautioned himself, striding to the door.

He had seen photographs, of course, and thought he knew what to expect of the woman waiting on the other side. But she was more delicate than he'd anticipated. Like fine lace that had been handled too carelessly, so that her skin was almost transparent and stretched too tightly over her fine bones, leaving her face much too small for her very blue eyes.

Standing back, he waved her across the threshold. "Signora Mallory, thank you for agreeing to see me. Please come in."

She hesitated a moment before complying. "I'm not aware you gave me much choice, Mr. Orsini," she said, her accent so vivid a reminder of Lindsay's that he was momentarily disconcerted. "Nor did I expect our meeting would take place in your room, and I can't say I'm particularly comfortable with that."

What did she think? That he'd traveled halfway around the world to seduce her? "My intentions are entirely honorable," he replied, tempted to tell her that if a romp in bed was all he wanted, he could have found it much closer to home.

She let him take her coat and shrugged, an elegantly

dismissive little gesture that made the pearls nested at her throat slither gently against her skin. "They'd better be," she said.

Suppressing a smile, he motioned to the array of bottles set out on the bar. "Will you join me in a drink before dinner?"

Again, she paused before inclining her head in assent. "A very weak wine spritzer, please."

"So," he said, adding a generous dollop of San Pellegrino to an inch of Pinot Grigio, and pouring a shot of whiskey for himself, "tell me about yourself, *signora*. I know only that you and my late wife were great friends, and that you are widowed, with a young son."

"Which is rather more than I know about you, Mr. Orsini," she replied, with a candor he found rather disarming. "And since I have absolutely no idea what this meeting is all about, I'd just as soon get down to business as waste time regaling you with a life history I'm sure you have no real interest in hearing about."

Joining her on the other side of the room, he handed her the spritzer and raised his own glass in a wordless toast. "That's where you're mistaken. Please understand that I have a most compelling and, indeed, legitimate reason for wanting to learn more about you."

"Fine. Then until you share that reason with me, please understand that I am not about to gratify your curiosity. I don't pretend to know how things are done in Sicily, but in this country, no woman with a grain of sense agrees to meet a strange man alone in his hotel room. Had I known that was your plan, I would most definitely not have come." She set her drink down on the coffee table and glanced very pointedly at her silver wristwatch. "You have exactly five minutes to explain yourself, Mr. Orsini, and then I'm out of here."

He took a sip of his whiskey and eyed her appraisingly. "I can see why you and my wife were such close friends. She, too, drove straight to the heart of a matter. It was one of the many qualities I admired in her."

"Four and a half minutes, Mr. Orsini, and I'm fast losing my patience."

"Very well." He picked up the leather folder he'd left on the coffee table and withdrew the letter. "This is for you. I think you'll find its contents self-explanatory."

She glanced briefly at the handwriting and paled. "It's from Lindsay."

"*Si.*"

"How do you know what it's about?"

"I read it."

A flush chased away her pallor. "Who gave you the right?"

"I did."

"Remind me never to leave private correspondence lying about when you're around," she said, her blue eyes flaring with indignation.

"Read your letter, *signora,* and then I will let you read mine. Perhaps when you've done that, you'll regard me with less hostility, and have a better understanding of why I came all this way to meet you."

She flung him one last doubtful glance, then bent her attention to the contents of the letter. At first, her hand was steady, but as she continued to read, the paper fluttered as if caught in the faintest of breezes, and by the time she reached the end, she was visibly shaking.

"Well, *signora?*"

She raised shocked eyes to his. "This is…ridiculous. She can't have been in her right mind."

"My wife was lucid to the last. Disease might have ravaged her body, but not her mind." He pushed his own letter across the table. "Here is what she asked of me. You'll notice both letters were written on the same day. Mine is a copy of the original. If you wish, you may keep it, to read again at your leisure."

Reluctantly Corinne Mallory took the second letter, scanned it quickly, then handed it back to him and shook her head in further disbelief. "I'm having a hard time accepting that Lindsay knew what she was asking."

"Yet viewed dispassionately, it makes a certain sense."

"Not to me it doesn't," she retorted flatly. "And I can't believe it does to you, either, or you'd have brought it to my attention sooner. These letters were written over three years ago. Why did you wait until now to tell me about them?"

"I accidentally discovered them myself only a few weeks ago. Lindsay had tucked them inside a photograph album, and I admit, on first reading, my reaction was much the same as yours."

"I hope you're not implying you're now in agreement with her wishes?"

"At the very least, they merit serious consideration."

Corinne Mallory rolled her big blue eyes and reached for her wineglass. "I might need something a bit stronger than this, after all."

"I understand the idea takes some getting used to, Signora Mallory, but I hope you won't dismiss it out of hand. From a purely practical standpoint, such an arrangement has much to recommend it."

"I've no wish to offend you, Mr. Orsini, but if you seriously believe that, I can't help thinking you must be a few bricks short of a full load."

"An interesting turn of phrase," he remarked, unable to suppress a smile, "but far from accurate, and I hope to persuade you of that over dinner."

"After reading these letters, I'm no longer sure dinner's such a good idea."

"Why not? Are you afraid I might sway you into changing your mind?"

"No," she said, with utter conviction.

"Then where's the harm in our discussing the matter over a good meal? If, at the end of it all, you're still of a mind to walk away, I certainly won't try to stop you. After all, the doubts cut two ways. At this point, I'm no more persuaded of the viability of my wife's request, than are you. But in honor of her memory, the very least I can do is put it to the test. She would expect no less of me—nor, I venture to point out, of you."

Corinne Mallory wrestled with herself for a moment or two, then heaved a sigh. "All right, I'll stay—for Lindsay's sake, because this meant so much to her. But please don't harbor any hope that I'll go along with her wishes."

He raised his glass again. "For Lindsay's sake," he agreed then, as a knock came at the door, gestured to the dining area situated in the corner. "That'll be our dinner. I ordered it served up here. Now that you realize the delicate nature of our business, I'm sure you agree it's not something to be conducted where others might overhear."

"I suppose not." Her reply signified agreement, but the hunted glance she cast around the suite suggested she was more interested in making a fast escape. "Is there some-place I can freshen up before we sit down?"

"Of course." He indicated the guest powder room at the end of the short hall leading past the kitchen and bedroom. "Take your time, *signora*. I expect the chef and his staff will need a few minutes to set everything up."

She'd need a lot more than a few minutes to pull herself together! Locking the powder room door, Corinne stared in the mirror over the long vanity unit, not surprised to find her cheeks flushed and her eyes feverishly bright. Emo-tionally she was under siege on all fronts, and had been from the second she'd arrived at Raffaello Orsini's door and come face-to-face with the most beautiful man she'd ever seen.

At the time of her wedding, Lindsay had sent photos, but that was years ago, and even if it had taken place just yes-terday, no camera could capture his raw sexual magnetism. A person had to view him in the flesh to appreciate that. For Corinne, the experience had almost put her in a trance.

He did not look the part in which she'd cast him. Yes, he had the smooth olive skin and gleaming black hair typical of someone Mediterranean born and bred, but as she understood it, Sicilian men did not, as a rule, stand over six feet tall, or sport a pair of shoulders that would do a football running back proud.

As for his face, she'd hardly been able to bring herself to look at it, afraid that if she did, she'd focus too intently on his sensuous mouth, rather than the words issuing from it, or lose herself in eyes the color of woodsmoke.

He'd rendered her tongue-tied, and for the first time,

she'd gained a glimmer of understanding for why Lindsay had so readily given up everything to be with him. That chiseled jaw, those exquisitely arrogant cheekbones and mesmerizing voice would have been hard to resist.

His hotel accommodation on the twenty-third floor was equally mind-boggling. A luxury suite, it was larger than most apartments, with a baby grand piano installed in the huge sitting room, seating for six at the round table in the dining alcove, and fabulous artwork on the walls. Not that she could imagine anyone paying much attention to the latter, at least not during the day, with stunning views of Stanley Park, Lions Gate Bridge, Coal Harbour and the North Shore mountains commanding attention beyond the windows.

Finally, and by far the most discombobulating, was the reason he'd asked her to meet him. If she hadn't recognized Lindsay's handwriting, she'd never have believed the letters were authentic. Even accepting that they were, she couldn't wrap her mind around their contents, which was why she'd tucked hers into her purse and brought it with her into the powder room.

Spreading it out on the vanity now, she prepared to read it again, this time without Raffaello Orsini's disturbing gaze tracking her every reaction.

June 12, 2005
Dear Corinne,
I hoped I'd see you one more time, and that we could talk, the way we've always been able to, without holding anything back. I hoped, too, that I'd be around to help Elisabetta celebrate her third birthday.

I know now that I'm not going to be here to do either of those things, and that I have very little time left to put my affairs in order. And so I'm forced to turn to writing, something which was never my strong suit.

Corinne, you've been widowed now for nearly a year, and I know better than anyone how hard it's been for you. I'm learning first-hand how painful grief can be, but to have money troubles on top of sorrow, as you continue to have, is more than anyone should have to put up with. At least I'm spared having to worry about that. But money can't buy health, nor can it compensate a child for losing a parent, something both your son and my daughter have to face. And that brings me to the point of this letter.

All children deserve two parents, Corinne. A mother to kiss away the little hurts, and to teach a daughter how to be a woman, and a son how to be tender. They also deserve a father to stand between them and a world which doesn't seem to differentiate between those able to cope with its senseless cruelties, and those too young to understand why it should be so.

I've known much happiness with Raffaello. He's a wonderful man, a wonderful role model for a young boy growing up without a father. He would be so good for your Matthew. And if I can't be there for my Elisabetta, I can think of no one I'd rather see taking my place than you, Corinne.

I've loved you practically from the day we met in second grade. You are my soul sister. So I'm asking you, please, to bring an open mind to my last wish, which is to see you and Raffaello join forces—and yes, I mean through marriage—and together fill the empty spaces in our children's lives.

You each have so much to bring to the arrangement, and so much to gain. But there's another reason that's not quite so unselfish. Elisabetta's too young to hold on to her memories of me, and I hate that. Raffaello will do his best to keep me alive in her heart, but no one knows me as well as you do. Only you can tell her what I was like as a child and a teenager. About my first big crush, my first heartbreak, my first kiss, my favorite book and movie and song, and so much more that I don't have time to list here.

It's enough to say that you and I share such a long and close history, and have never kept secrets from each other. Having you to turn to would give her the next best thing to me.

I'd trust you with my life, Corinne, but it's not worth anything now, so I'm trusting you with my daughter's instead. I want so badly to live, and I'm so afraid of dying, but I think I could face it more easily if I knew you and Raffaello…

The letter ended there, the handwriting not as sure, as if Lindsay had run out of the strength required to continue. Or perhaps she'd been too blinded by the tears, which had blurred the last few lines and left watery stains on the paper—stains made even larger by Corinne's own tears now.

Desperate to keep her grief private, she flushed the toilet, hoping the sound would disguise the sobs tearing at her, then mopped at her face with a handful of tissues. She didn't need to look in the mirror to know her makeup was ruined. The mascara stung her eyes, adding insult to injury.

"Oh, Lindsay," she mourned softly, "you know I'd do anything for you…anything at all. Except this."

CHAPTER TWO

SHE RETURNED to the main room to find the moon casting an icy swath across the ink-black waters of the harbor. Within the suite, a floor lamp poured a pool of warm yellow light over the love seat next to the window, but at the linen-draped dining table, candles now shimmered over the crystal and silverware, and lent a more subtle blush to a centerpiece of cream roses. She was glad of that. Candlelight was much kinder, its subdued glow helping to disguise her reddened eyes, bereft now of any trace of mascara.

Raffaello Orsini held out her chair before taking a seat opposite, and nodding permission for the hovering waiter to pour the wine, a very fine sparkling white burgundy. Still shaken from rereading Lindsay's letter, Corinne could barely manage a taste, and was sure she'd never be able to swallow a bite of food. She deeply regretted having accepted her host's imperious invitation. Quite apart from the fact that her composure lay in shreds, she knew she looked a mess, and what woman was ever at her sharpest under those circumstances?

At least he had the good grace not to comment on her appearance, or her initial lack of response to his conversation. Instead, as braised endive salad followed a first course of crab and avocado pâté served on toast points, with foie gras-stuffed quail bathed in a sherry vinaigrette as the entrée, he regaled her with an amusing account of his tourist experiences earlier in the day. And almost without her realizing, she was coaxed into doing at least some justice to a meal he'd clearly taken great pains to make as appealing as possible.

By the time dessert arrived, a wonderful silky chocolate mousse she couldn't resist, a good deal of her tension had melted away. The man oozed confidence, and reeked not so much of wealth, although he clearly had money to burn, but of the power that went with it. A heady combination, she had to admit. Watching him, enjoying his dry wit and keen observations, and more than a little dazzled by the smile he allowed so sparingly, she was almost able to push aside the real reason for their meeting and pretend, just for a little while, that they were merely a man and woman enjoying an evening together.

Lulled into a comfortable haze induced by candlelight, and a voice whose exotic cadence suggested an intimacy worth discovering, if only she dared, she almost relaxed. He was a complex man; an intriguing contradiction in terms. His wafer-thin Patek Philippe watch, handmade shoes and flawlessly tailored suit belonged to a CEO, a chairman of the board, a tycoon at his best wheeling and dealing megamillions in the arena of international business. Yet the contained strength of his body suggested he could sling a goat over one shoulder and scale a Sicilian mountainside without breaking a sweat. Despite that, though, there was absolutely nothing of the rustic in him. He was sophistication personified, and much too charming and handsome for his own good.

Or hers. Because, like a hawk luring a mouse into the open, he suddenly struck, diving in for the kill before she realized she'd left herself vulnerable to him. "So far, I've done all the talking, *signora*. Now it's your turn. So tell me, please, what is there about you that I might find noteworthy?"

"Not much, I'm afraid," she said, disconcerted by the question, but not yet suspecting where it would lead. "I'm a single, working parent, with very little time to do anything noteworthy."

"Too occupied with making ends meet, you mean?"

"That about covers it, yes."

"What kind of work do you do?"

"I'm a professional chef."

"Ah, yes. I remember now that my wife once mentioned that. You were snapped up by a five-star restaurant in the city, as I recall."

"Before my marriage, yes. After that, I was a stay-at-home wife and mother. When my husband died, I...needed extra income, so I opened a small catering company."

"You're now self-employed, then?"

"Yes."

"You hire others to help you?"

"Not always. At first, I could handle the entire workload alone. Now that my clientele has increased, I do bring in extra help on occasion, but still do most of the food preparation myself."

"And offer a very exclusive service to your patrons, I'm sure."

"Yes. They expect me to oversee special events in person."

"A demanding business, being one's own boss, don't you find? What prompted you to tackle such an undertaking?"

"It allowed me to be at home with my son when he was a baby."

"Resourceful and enterprising. I admire that in a woman." He steepled his fingers and regarded her sympathetically. "How do you find it, now that your son's older?"

"It's not so easy," she admitted. "He's long past the age where he's content to play quietly in a corner while I create a wedding buffet for sixty people."

He allowed himself a small, sympathetic smile. "I don't doubt it. So who looks after him when you're away taking care of the social needs of strangers?"

"My next-door neighbor," she replied, wincing inwardly at his too-accurate assessment of her clientele. "She's an older woman, a widow and a grandmother, and very reliable."

"But not quite as devoted to him as you are, I'm sure."

"Is anyone ever able to take a mother's place, Mr. Orsini?"

"No, as I have learned to my very great cost." Then switching subjects suddenly, he said, "What sort of place do you live in?"

Bristling, she snapped, "Not a hovel, if that's what you're implying," and wondered how much Lindsay had told him about her straitened circumstances.

"I didn't suggest that it was," he returned mildly. "I'm merely trying to learn more about you. Paint the appropriate background to a very attractive portrait, if you like."

Mollified enough to reply less defensively, she said, "I rent a two-bedroom town house in a gated community several miles south of the city."

"In other words, a safe place where your son can play in the garden without fear that he might wander away."

She thought of the narrow patio outside her kitchen, the strip of lawn not much bigger than a bath towel that lay beyond it and her neighbors on the other side, the Shaws—a crusty old couple in their eighties, who complained constantly that Matthew made too much noise. "Not exactly. I have no garden as such. I take him to play at a nearby park instead, and if I'm not available, my sitter takes him for me."

"But there are other children he can visit in this gated community, boys his own age, with similar interests?"

"Unfortunately not. Most residents are older—many, like my baby-sitter, retired."

"Does he at least have a dog or cat to keep him company?"

"We aren't allowed to own pets."

He raised his elegant black brows. "*Dio,* he might as well be in prison, for all the freedom he enjoys."

In truth, she couldn't refute an opinion which all too closely coincided with her own, but she wasn't about to tell him so. "Nothing's ever perfect, Mr. Orsini. If it were, our children wouldn't be growing up with one parent standing in for two."

"But they are," he replied. "Which brings me to my next question. Now that you've had time to recover from the initial shock, what is your opinion on the content of the letters?"

"What?" She raised startled eyes to his and found herself impaled in a gaze at once penetrating and inscrutable.

"Your opinion," he repeated, a sudden hint of steel threading his words. "Surely, Signora Mallory, you haven't forgotten the real reason you're here?"

"Hardly. I just haven't given the matter…much thought."

"Then I suggest you do so. Enough time has passed since my wife wrote of her last wishes. I do not propose to delay honoring them any longer than I have to."

"Well, I do not propose to be bullied, Mr. Orsini, not by you or anyone else. Since you're so anxious for an answer, though, let me be blunt. I can't see myself ever agreeing to Lindsay's request."

"Her friendship meant so little to you, then?"

"Save the emotional blackmail for someone else," she shot back. "It's not going to work with me."

His smoky-gray eyes darkened. With suppressed anger? Sorrow? Frustration? She couldn't tell. His expression gave away nothing. "Emotion does not play a role in this situation. It is a business proposition, pure and simple, devised solely for the benefit of your child and mine. The most convenient way to implement it is for you and me to join forces in marriage."

"Something I find totally unacceptable. In case you're not aware, marriages of convenience went out of fashion in this country a long time ago. Should I ever decide to marry again, which is doubtful, it will be to someone of my own choosing."

"It seems to me, Signora Mallory, that you're in no position to be so particular. By your own admission, you do not own your own home, which leaves you at the mercy of a landlord, you're overworked and your son spends a great deal of time being cared for by someone other than yourself."

"At least I have my independence."

"For which both you and your boy pay a very high price." He regarded her silently a moment, then in a seductively cajoling tone, went on, "I admire your spirit, *cara mia,* but why are you so set on continuing with your present lifestyle, when I can offer you so much more?"

"For a start, because I don't like having charity forced down my throat." *And calling me* cara mia *isn't going to change that.*

"Is that how you see this? Do you not understand that, in our situation, the favors work both ways—that my daughter stands to gain as much from the arrangement as your son?"

Absently Corinne touched a fingertip to the velvet-soft petals of the nearest rose. They reminded her of Matthew's skin when he was a baby. Before he'd turned into a tyrant.

...Raffaello will do his best to keep me alive in her heart, but having you to turn to would be the next best thing to having me, Lindsay had written, or words to that effect. *I'm entrusting you with my daughter's life, Corinne....*

Seeming to think she was actually considering his proposal, Raffaello Orsini asked, "Are you afraid I'm going to demand my husbandly rights in the bedroom?"

"I don't know. Are you?" Corinne blurted out rashly, too irked by the faint hint of derision in his question to consider how he might interpret her reply.

"Would you like me to?"

She opened her mouth to issue a flat denial, then snapped it closed as an image swam unbidden into her mind, shockingly detailed, shockingly erotic, of how Raffaello Orsini's naked body might look. Her inner response—the jolt of awareness that rocked her body, the sudden flush of heat streaming through her blood—appalled her.

She'd moved through the preceding four years like an automaton, directing all her energies to providing a safe, stable and loving home for her son. As breadwinner, the one responsible for everything from rent to medical insurance to paying off debts incurred by her late husband, she'd had no choice but to put her own needs aside. To be assaulted now by this sudden aberration—for how else could she describe it?—was ridiculous, but also an untimely reminder that she was still a woman whose sexuality might have been relegated to the back burner, but whose flame, it seemed, had not been entirely extinguished.

"Don't feel you have to make up your mind on that point at this very moment," Orsini suggested smoothly. "The welfare of two children is the main issue here, not sexual intercourse between you and me. I shall not press you to consummate the marriage against your will, but you're an attractive woman and as a hot-blooded Sicilian, I would not spurn your overtures, should you feel inclined to make any."

Hot-blooded Sicilian, maybe, she thought, staggered by his arrogance, but it'll be a cold day in hell before I come begging for sexual favors from you. "There's not the slightest chance of that ever happening, for the simple reason that I have no intention at all of agreeing to your proposition. It's a lousy idea."

"Why? What's wrong with two adults uniting to create a semblance of normal family life for their children? Don't you think they deserve it?"

"They deserve the best that we can give them—and that is *not* by having their respective parents marry for all the wrong reasons."

"That would be true only if we were deluding ourselves into believing our hearts are engaged, *signora,* which they most certainly are not. Rather, we're approaching this from a cerebral angle. And that, in my opinion, vastly increases our chances of making the union work."

"*Cerebral?*" She almost choked on her after-dinner coffee. "Is that how you'd define it?"

"How else? After all, it's not as if either of us is looking for love in a second marriage, both of us having lost our true soul mates, the first time around. We harbor no romantic illusions. We're simply entering into a binding contract to improve our children's lives."

Unnerved as much by his logic as his unremitting gaze, she left the table and went to stand at the window. "You omit to mention the extent to which I would benefit financially from such an arrangement."

"I hardly consider it important enough to merit attention."

"It is to me."

"Why? Because you feel you're being bought?"

"Among other things, yes."

"That's ridiculous."

She shrugged. "Finally we agree on something. In fact, the whole idea's preposterous. People don't get married for such reasons."

"Why do they get married?"

Beleaguered by his relentless inquisition, she floundered for a reply and came up with exactly the wrong one. "Well, as you already made clear. For love."

Yet in the end, at least for her, life had rubbed off all the magic, and what she'd believed was love had turned out to be lust. Infatuation. Make-believe. An illusion. The only good thing to come out of her marriage had been Matthew, and if Joe had lived, she knew with certainty that they'd have ended up in divorce court.

From across the room, Raffaello Orsini's hypnotic voice drifted into the silence, weaving irresistible word pictures. "You would be marrying for love this time, too. For love of your son. Think about him, *cara mia*. Hear his laughter as he runs and plays with a companion, in acres of gardens. Imagine him building sand castles on a safe, secluded beach, or learning to swim in warm, crystal clear waters. See yourself living in a spacious villa, with no monetary cares and all the time in the world to devote to your child. Then tell me, if you dare, that our joining forces is such a bad idea."

He was offering Matthew more than she could ever hope to provide, and although pride urged her not to be swayed by what was, in effect, a blatant bribe, as a mother she had to ask herself if she had the right to deprive her son of a better life. Yet to sell herself to the highest bidder... what kind of woman did that make her?

Torn, confused, she considered her options.

Money could buy just about anything, and it was all very fine for high-minded people to scorn it as the root of all evil, but until they found themselves having to scrape and save every last cent in order to make ends meet, they were in no position to cast judgment on those who faced just such a situation every day.

On the other hand, it was claimed by those who ought to know that there were never any free lunches, and if something seemed too good to be true, it probably was. The kind of lopsided bargain Raffaello Orsini was proposing might well end up costing more than it was worth. Would she really be doing Matthew any favors if she ended up losing her self-respect?

Marshaling her thoughts, she said, "You've gone to

great pains to explain how the arrangement might benefit me, Mr. Orsini, but exactly what's in it for you?"

From the corner of her eye, she saw him go to the bar and pour cognac into two brandy snifters. "When Lindsay died," he replied, joining her at the window and passing one glass to her, "my mother and aunt moved into my house, to take care of Elisabetta and, if I'm to speak with truth, to take care of me, too. It's as well that they did. At the time, I was too angry, too wrapped up in my own grief, to be the kind of father my daughter deserved. These two good women put their own lives on hold and devoted themselves to ours."

"You were very lucky that they were there when you needed them."

He swirled his brandy and warmed the bowl of the glass between his hands. "Very lucky, yes, and very grateful, too."

She heard the reservation in his tone and glanced at him sharply. "But?"

"But they have indulged Elisabetta to the point that she is becoming unmanageable, and I am at a loss to know how to put a stop to that without hurting their feelings. She needs a consistently firm hand, Corinne, and I am not doing such a good job of providing one, in part because the demands of my work take me away from home at times, but also because…" He shrugged ruefully. "I am a man."

His use of her first name left Corinne giddy with such insane pleasure that she lost all control over her tongue. "So I've noticed." Then appalled at how he might interpret her answer, she rushed to explain, "What I mean is, that like most of your breed, you seem to think because you decree something, it shall be done."

He actually laughed at that, the sound as rich and dark as buckwheat honey, then just as suddenly sobered. "You've read Lindsay's letters. You know what she wanted. What you can do for me, Corinne, is carry out her dying wishes. Take her place in Elisabetta's life. Shape my daughter into the kind of woman that would make her mother proud.

"It will be no easy task, I assure you, so if, as I suspect, you think I'm the one doing all the giving, please think again. What I offer to you can, for the most part, be measured in euros. It is impossible to put a price on what you have to offer to me."

"You're very persuasive, Mr. Orsini, but the fact remains, logistics alone make the idea impractical on any number of fronts."

"Name one."

"I signed a three-year lease on my town house."

"I will break it for you."

"I have obligations…debts."

"I will discharge them."

"I don't want your money."

"You need my money."

He had an answer for everything. At her wit's end, she took a different tack. "What if you don't like my son?"

"Are you likely to dislike my daughter?"

"Of course not. She's just a child. An innocent little girl."

His raised hand, palm facing up, spoke more eloquently than words. "Exactly. Our children are the innocents, and we their appointed guardians."

"You'd expect me to disrupt my son's life and move to Sicily."

"What is there to keep you here? Your parents?"

Hardly. Their disenchantment with her had begun when she was still in her teens.

A chef? they'd sneered, when Corinne had shared her ambitions with them. *Is slaving over a hot stove all day the best you can aspire to after the kind of education we've given you? What will people think?*

But that was nothing compared to their reaction when Joe entered the picture. *Marry that fly-boy Joe Mallory, young lady, and you're on your own,* her father had threatened.

Determined to have the last word as usual, her mother had added, *Your father's right. But then, you never did use the brains God gave you, otherwise you'd have chosen that nice accountant you were dating last year, before he got tired of being strung along and ended up marrying someone else.*

That they'd ultimately been proved right about Joe did nothing to lessen Corinne's sense of abandonment. She couldn't imagine ever turning her back on Matthew. Parents just didn't do that to their children. But hers had, and shown not a speck of remorse about it.

"No," she told Raffaello Orsini. "They retired to Arizona and we seldom visit."

"You are estranged?"

"More or less," she admitted, but didn't elaborate.

He closed the small distance between them and with a touch to her shoulder swung her round to face him. "Then all the more reason for you to marry me. I come with instant family."

"I don't speak Italian."

"You will learn, and so will your boy."

"Your mother and aunt might resent a stranger coming into the household and taking over."

"My mother and aunt will accede to my wishes."

Once again, he had an answer for everything. "Stop badgering me!" she cried, desperation lending an edge of hysteria to her voice. No matter how real the obstacles she flung in his path, he steamrolled over it and confronted her with an even better reason why she, too, should *accede to his wishes*. And if she didn't put a stop to him now, she'd end up surrendering to his demands from sheer battle fatigue.

"*Ti prego, pardonami*—forgive me. You're in shock, as was I when I first read my wife's letters, and for me to expect you to reach a decision at once is both unreasonable and inexcusable."

His response, uttered with heartfelt regret, so far undermined her battered defenses that, to her horror, she heard herself say. "Exactly. I need some time to assimilate the benefits and the drawbacks, and I can't do it with you breathing down my neck."

"I absolutely understand." He strode to the desk, returned with an envelope containing several photographs, which he spilled onto the coffee table. "Perhaps these will help clarify matters for you. Would you like me to leave you alone for a few minutes so that you may examine them?"

"No," she said firmly. "I would like to go home and take my time reaching a decision, without the pressure of knowing you're hovering in the background."

"How much time? I must return to Sicily as soon as possible."

"I'll have an answer for you tomorrow." In all truth, she

had an answer for him now, but it wasn't the one he wanted to hear, so she might as well keep it to herself and make her escape while she could. The sooner she put distance between him and her, the less likely she was to find herself agreeing to something she knew was out of the question.

"Fair enough." He slid the photographs back into their envelope, tucked it in the inside pocket of his jacket, then retrieved her coat and, after draping it around her shoulders, picked up the phone. "Give me a moment to alert the driver that we're ready for him."

"You don't need to come down with me," she said, after he'd made the call. "I can find my own way."

"I'm sure you can, Corinne," he replied. "You strike me as a woman who can do just about anything she puts her mind to. But I will accompany you nevertheless."

All the way back to her town house? She sincerely hoped not. Bad enough that his effect on her was such that she hadn't been able to issue an outright refusal to his ludicrous proposition. The enforced intimacy of a forty-minute drive with him in the back of a dark limousine, and there was no telling what she might end up saying.

As it turned out, he had no such intention. He walked her through the lobby and out to where the limousine waited, handed her into the backseat then, at the last minute, withdrew the envelope from his pocket and dropped it in her lap. "*Buena notte,* Corinne," he murmured, pinning her in his mesmerizing gaze. "I look forward to hearing from you tomorrow."

CHAPTER THREE

SHE FLUNG HIM a baleful look and tried to return the envelope to him, but the wretched thing fell open and released its contents, which slithered in disarray over the leather upholstery. By the time she'd scooped them up, the door had clicked shut and the car was moving smoothly into the downtown traffic.

Wearily—she seemed to have been fighting one thing or another ever since the evening began, starting with Matthew's tantrum at once again being left in Mrs. Lehman's care—Corinne stuffed the photographs into her purse. Just because Raffaello Orsini had decreed that she should accept them didn't mean she had to look at them, did it? She'd send them back to him by courier tomorrow, along with her rejection of his proposal.

When the limousine driver at last dropped her off at the entrance to the town house complex, she knew a sense of relief. It might not be much by most people's standards, especially not the obscenely rich Mr. Orsini's, but it was home, and all that mattered most in the world to her lay under its roof. Hugging her coat collar close against the freezing night air, she hurried to her front door, her heels ringing like iron on the concrete driveway she shared with her neighbors.

Once inside the house, she realized at once that it was too quiet. As a rule, Mrs. Lehman watched television in the family room adjoining the kitchen, and being a little hard of hearing, turned up the volume. But tonight, she met Corinne in the tiny entrance hall, her own front door key in her hand, as if she couldn't wait to vacate the premises. In itself, this was unusual enough, but what really dismayed Corinne was the dried blood and ugly bruise already discoloring the baby-sitter's cheekbone, just below her left eye.

Dropping her purse on the floor, Corinne rushed forward for a closer look. "Good heavens, Mrs. Lehman, what happened? And where are your glasses? Did you fall?"

"No, dear." Normally the most forthright of women, she refused to meet Corinne's gaze. "My glasses got broken."

"How? Oh…!" Sudden awful premonition sent Corinne's stomach plummeting. "Oh, please tell me Matthew isn't responsible!"

"Well, yes, I'm afraid he is. We had a bit of a run-in about his bedtime, you see, and…he threw one of his toy trucks at me. It was after ten before he finally settled down."

Corinne felt physically ill. She'd spent the evening being wined and dined with the very best, by a man she'd never met before, and for what? A proposition so absurd it didn't merit a second thought. And meanwhile, her son was abusing the kindness of the one woman she most relied on to help her out when she needed it.

"I hardly know what to say, Mrs. Lehman. An apology

just doesn't cut it." Then, biting her lip at her poor choice of words, she examined the cut more closely. It had stopped bleeding and didn't appear to be deep, but it must be sore. "Is there anything I can get for you? Some ice, perhaps?"

"No, dear, thank you. I'd just like to get to my own bed, if you don't mind."

"Come on, then. I'll walk you home." Taking her arm, Corinne steered her gently to the door.

"Don't trouble yourself, Corinne. It's only a few yards. I can manage by myself."

But Corinne waved aside her objections. Frost sparkled on the path, and she wasn't taking a chance on the poor woman slipping and breaking a hip. Enough damage had been done for one night. "I insist. And tomorrow, Matthew and I will be over to see you—after I've dealt with him, that is."

She barely slept that night for worrying. What if Mrs. Lehman's injury was worse than it looked, and she suffered a concussion? Lapsed into a coma? What if her sight had been damaged? She'd claimed not to have a headache, had seemed steady enough on her feet during the short walk to her front door and had no trouble inserting the key in the lock, but she was well into her seventies and at that age…

Aware she was letting her imagination run riot, Corinne focused on the underlying cause of so much angst. What was happening to her son, that he would behave so badly? A "run-in," Mrs. Lehman had called it, but in Corinne's estimation, broken glasses and a black eye amounted to a lot more than that.

Yet if she was brutally honest with herself, she shouldn't be altogether surprised. Lately she'd come close to a few such "run-ins" herself. How did she put a stop to them before they escalated beyond all control and something *really* serious happened?

Finally, around four in the morning, she fell into an uneasy sleep riddled with dreams in which all the town houses in the complex fell down. Mrs. Lehman rode away in a big black limousine with every stick of her furniture piled next to her on the backseat. Corinne fought her way out of the rubble that she'd once called home, to look for Matthew who was lost, and came face-to-face with Raffaello Orsini shuffling a deck of playing cards. "This is all your house was made of, *signora*," he said, fanning them out for her to see. "You have nothing."

She awoke just after eight, her pulse racing, to find that some time while she slept, Matthew had left his own bed and now lay curled up beside her, safe and sound, and such a picture of innocence that her heart contracted in her breast.

She loved him more than life; too much, she sometimes thought, to be a really effective disciplinarian. When things went horribly wrong, as they had last night, the full brunt of being the only parent weighed heavily on her conscience. Yet she knew that, had he lived, Joe would have sloughed off his share of that responsibility, just as he had every other. He'd been no more cut out for fatherhood than he had for marriage.

Dreading the morning ahead, she inched out of bed, showered and dressed in comfortable fleece sweatpants and top, and went down to the kitchen to prepare breakfast. Should she make her son pancakes, as she'd promised, she wondered, or would that be condoning his bad behavior? Did his transgression justify her breaking her word? Did two wrongs ever make a right?

She was still debating the matter when Matthew came downstairs, trailing his blanket behind him, and climbed up on the stool at the breakfast bar. He looked such a waif, with his hair sticking out every which way, and one side of his face imprinted with the creases in his bedding, that her heart melted.

Okay, pancakes but no blueberries, she decided, pouring him a glass of juice. And for her, coffee, very strong. She needed a jolt of caffeine to drive the gritty residue of too little sleep from her eyes and give her the boost she needed to face what lay ahead.

Overnight, the sky had turned leaden. A persistent drizzle shrouded the trees in mist and reached its damp aura past the ill-fitting window over the sink to infiltrate the house. Next door, Mrs. Shaw screeched for Mr. Shaw to come and get his oatmeal before it grew cold. In Corinne's own kitchen, Matthew, also out of sorts from too little sleep, stabbed his fork into his pancakes and spattered himself with syrup.

Steeling herself to patience, she waited until he'd finished his meal before tackling him about the previous night. As she expected, the conversation did not go well.

"I don't have to," he said, when she scolded him for not obeying Mrs. Lehman. "She's not my mommy. She's silly." Then, sliding down from the stool, he announced, "I'm going to play with my trains and horses now."

Swiftly Corinne corralled him and hauled him back to his seat. "You most certainly are not, young man. You're going to listen to me, then after you're dressed, we're going next door and you're going to tell Mrs. Lehman you're sorry you hurt her."

"No," he said, aiming a kick at her shin. "You're silly, as well."

Barely nine o'clock, and already time-out time, she thought wearily. But when she went to take him back to his room, he turned limp as a piece of spaghetti, slumped on the floor and burst into tears. He was still screaming when the doorbell rang. Leaving him to it, Corinne trudged to answer.

Mrs. Lehman stood outside, her eye almost lost in the swelling around it, her bruise a magnificent shade of purple. "No, dear, I won't come in, thank you," she said in response to Corinne's invitation. "I'm going to stay with my married daughter, to give her a hand with the new baby, and she'll be here any minute to pick me up."

"That's nice," Corinne said, hardly able to look at the poor woman, her face was such a mess. "But you should just have phoned, Mrs. Lehman, instead of coming out in this weather. And if you're worried about looking after Matthew, please don't be. Business is always slow in January, and I'm sure I can—"

"Yes, well, about that. I'm afraid I won't be looking after him anymore, dear, because I'm not going to be living next door much longer. My daughter and her husband have been after me for months to move in with them, and I've decided to take them up on it. That's why I came over. You've always been very kind to me, and I wanted to tell you to your face. And give you back your key."

"I see." And Corinne did, all too clearly. The episode last night had been the last straw. "I'm so sorry, Mrs. Lehman," she said miserably. "I feel as if we're driving you out of your home."

"Oh, rubbish! The plain fact is, there's nothing to keep

me here since I lost my husband, and I've been ready for a move for some time now. And truth to tell, even if I wasn't, I couldn't have continued baby-sitting your boy much longer. He's got more energy than he knows what to do with, and I'm past the age where I can keep up with him." A wry smile crossed her face as Matthew's wails echoed through the house. "Anyway, I'd better let you get back to him. From the sound of it, you've got your hands full this morning."

Just then, a car drew up outside her door. "There's my daughter now, and I've still to pack a few things to see me through the next day or two," she said, and thrust a slip of paper in Corinne's hand. "Here's what you owe me. Just drop a check in my mailbox, and I'll collect it when I come to get the rest of my stuff." She bathed Corinne in a fond, sad smile. "Goodbye, dear, and all the best."

Corinne watched as the daughter climbed out of her car. Heard the younger woman's shocked exclamation at the sight of her mother. Saw the outraged glare she directed at Corinne. Never more ashamed or embarrassed than she was at that moment, Corinne slunk back inside the house, shut her own front door and retraced her steps to the kitchen.

She found Matthew quite recovered from his tantrum and happily playing with his trains and horses. She wished she could leave it at that, let last night's incident go and just move on. But young though he might be, he had to be held accountable for his actions. And if she didn't teach him that, who would?

Sighing, she waded in to what she knew would be a battle royal. Tried reason in the face of defiance; calm in the midst of storm. Nothing worked. He resisted her at every turn, flinging himself on the floor, giving vent to his frustration at the top of his lungs.

He broke her heart with his tears and anger. What had happened to her sunny-tempered little boy, that he was now in his room for a "time-out," when he should have been enjoying himself?

She knew what. He needed a full-time mother, and she couldn't give him one. And the fact that she was doing the best she could under trying circumstances did nothing to ease her conscience. Something had to change, and fast, but what—and how?

Pouring a fresh cup of coffee, she paced the confines of her kitchen and considered her options. She could hire extra staff for her business and spend more time at home with her son. But not only was good help hard to find, it didn't come cheap, and money was a perennial problem. Had been ever since Joe died and her credit rating had hit the skids because of the debts he'd run up on their jointly held accounts.

Shortly after his death, the bank had foreclosed on their mortgage and she'd lost the house. She'd been forced to leave the upscale suburban neighborhood with its acred lots and treed avenues, where Matthew had been born and just about everyone else on the street had young families. Had had to trade in her safe, reliable car for a twelve-year-old van, large enough to hold her catering supplies, certainly, but with such a history of abuse that she never knew when it might let her down. In a bid to avoid bankruptcy, she'd cut all her expenses to the bone, yet had to splurge on supplies to give her fledgling catering company a fighting chance of success.

But although she might be the one caught in a vicious financial bind, in the end, Matthew was the one paying the real price, and how high that price might go didn't bear thinking about.

We don't have fun together anymore, she thought sorrowfully. *I used to play with him. Sing to him. Make him laugh. Now I make him cry, and I can't remember the last time I really laughed until my stomach ached.*

She used to do other things, too, like look forward to tomorrow, and wring every drop of enjoyment out of life. Now she woke up and wondered how she'd get through the day. She was afraid all the time, waiting for the other shoe to drop.

What sort of message did that send to Matthew?

Our children are the innocents, Raffaello Orsini had said last night.

Raffaello Orsini… Even the silent mention of his name was enough for him to fill the house with his invisible presence; his implacable logic.

Think about your boy….

What's wrong with a binding contract to improve our children's lives…don't they deserve it?

Involuntarily her glance swung to the table in the dining nook where she'd tossed the envelope he'd given her. Exercising a mind of their own, her feet followed suit. She sat down. Picked up the envelope. Dared to examine its contents.

She discovered pictures of a villa, its rooms cooled by whirring fans and dressed in soothing shades of oyster-white and dove-gray and soft blue. Original oil paintings hung on its walls, antique rugs covered its pale marble floors, elaborate wrought-iron grilles accented its elegant curved windows, and frescoes its high domed ceilings.

Lindsay's kind of house: spacious, airy and charming. And outside its ancient stone walls, palm trees and flower beds filled with vivid color, and emerald-green lawns as smooth as velvet, and a distant view of turquoise seas.

Slowly Corinne lifted her gaze and looked at her present surroundings, at the place Matthew called home. The town house was too old to be sought after, and not nearly old enough to be chic. The rooms were poky and, on days like today, dark; the walls so paper thin that, at night, she could hear Mr. Shaw snoring in bed, next door.

She thought of Matthew being confined to a square of patio barely large enough to hold a sandbox, and much too small for him to ride his trike. She remembered last summer when Mrs. Shaw had vehemently accused him of kicking his soccer ball and breaking the plastic planter holding her geraniums. "Keep that brat on his own side of the property," she'd snapped.

Corinne thought of his never having play dates because no other children lived close by. Of his constantly being told not to make noise because he might disturb the neighbors. Little boys were supposed to make noise. They were supposed to run and play themselves into happy exhaustion. But his life was bound by other people's rules and expectations to the point that he was like a tender young plant, so deprived of light and water that it couldn't thrive.

Viewed from that perspective, Lindsay's request no longer seemed quite as far-fetched as it had upon first reading. "A business proposition, pure and simple, devised solely for the benefit of your child and mine," Raffaello Orsini had called it.

If, as he'd maintained, emotion wasn't allowed to enter the picture, could they make it work? And if so, what would it be like to look forward to tomorrow, instead of dreading what it might bring? For that matter, when was the last time she'd looked forward to anything except getting through each day the best way she knew how?

The question brought her up short. With an attitude like hers, was it any wonder Matthew misbehaved? Her own disenchantment had spilled over onto him. But now, suddenly, the power to change all that lay within her grasp.

Horrified, she realized her resolve to turn down Raffaello Orsini's proposal was weakening, and as if to drive the final nail in the coffin of her resistance, one last photograph fell out of the envelope and held her transfixed. Unlike the others, it had nothing to do with luxury or locale. This time, the camera had recorded the face of a little girl.

Although the date in the corner showed the picture had been taken within the last six months, the face was Lindsay's all over again. The vivacious smile, the eyes, and the dimples were hers. Only the hair was different; darker, thicker, springier.

I'm trusting you with my daughter's life, Corinne... having you to turn to would give her the next best thing to me....

Corinne traced a fingertip over the delicate features of the girl in the photograph. "Elisabetta," she breathed, on a soft sigh of defeat.

Patience was not his strong suit, at least not when it came to matters of business. And the proposal he'd put before

Corinne Mallory last night was entirely concerned with business. Surely a woman of reason could quickly ascertain that the pros vastly outweighed the cons? Yet here it was, almost four o'clock, and still no response from her.

Deciding he'd waited long enough, he picked up the phone. Then, about to punch in her number, he abruptly changed his mind, called the hotel's front desk instead and ordered a car and driver. Slightly more than an hour later, with daylight fading fast, he was at her town house.

That he was the last person she expected to find on her doorstep became immediately apparent when she answered his ring. "What are you doing here?" she inquired, so flustered she could barely articulate the question.

"I would prefer not to be," he replied. "Indeed, had you seen fit to contact me as you promised, I would have spared myself the trouble. But, they say, do they not, that if the mountain will not come to the man, then the man must come to the mountain? Not," he added, eyeing her too-slender frame judiciously, "that I consider you to match the proportions of such a land mass, but you are, it would seem, equally immovable."

"You've got it backward, Mr. Orsini. It's 'if the man won't come to the mountain, then the mountain must come to him.' And if you'd waited a bit longer, you could have saved yourself the trouble." She waved a large envelope in his face. "I have your answer here. In fact, when I heard someone buzzing to be let through the gates, I assumed it was the courier come to collect it."

"Well, since I have no intention of leaving empty-handed, you'd better call and cancel the pickup," he said.

"I suppose I'd better." She shifted her weight from one

foot to the other. "And I suppose, since you're here anyway, we might as well get this over with. Please come in."

Her demeanor suggested she'd rather invite a plague of rats into her household. *"Grazie tante,"* he said, with more than a touch of irony.

She led the way down a short hall to a kitchen, and went immediately to the telephone, leaving him free to look around. At one end of the room, separated by a high breakfast counter, was a sitting area of sorts, with a glass door looking out on what appeared to be a dismally small area which he supposed comprised her garden. A floor lamp, a television set on a stand, a shelf unit crammed with children's books and puzzles, and a two-seater couch and armchair separated by an occasional table, made up the furnishings, with what he thought might be a toy box in the corner.

Yellow paint on the walls, a rather fine old rug on the floor and a vase of pale daffodils on the counter added bright touches of warmth and comfort, while a cake cooling on a rack beside the stove filled the air with spicy fragrance. But although she was obviously a woman of taste and had made the place as charming as possible, it struck him as barely adequate and a world removed from the comfort he could provide.

Had she looked at the photographs he'd given her, and arrived at the same conclusion? Curious to know, he took a seat on a high stool at the counter and went to pick up the courier envelope she'd left there. But, ending her phone call, she forestalled him and snatched it out of his reach.

"Now that you're here, we can dispense with that and talk face-to-face," she said.

"As you wish."

"I just made tea. Would you like some?"

"I'd prefer to get down to the matter between us. After, if there is occasion to do so, we can linger over tea."

"Very well." She cleared her throat and flung him a harried glance. "After much thought and soul searching, I've decided to accept your offer."

In the business world, he was renowned for his poker face; for his ability to hide his emotions and reactions so proficiently that his associates never could tell where they stood in negotiations with him. But she, in a few succinct words, came close to stripping his inner feelings bare.

Collecting himself with difficulty, he said, "I was expecting a different answer."

"Are you disappointed?"

"Surprised, certainly, but not disappointed, no." He regarded her closely, noting again the fine texture of her skin, the lush fringe of lashes shielding her very blue eyes and the thick, shining mass of her hair, which she wore loosely tied back today. "Last night, you left me with the impression that nothing could persuade you in my favor. What changed your mind?"

"My son." She fixed him in a candid stare. "Let me be very frank with you, Mr. Orsini. If there was any way I could afford to turn you down, I would do so. But I looked through your photographs and have a pretty good idea of your standard of living. And you've seen enough of this house to draw your own conclusions about mine. Last night, you said that this is all about the children, and you were right. If, by selling myself to you, I can provide Matthew with a better life, then that's what I'm willing to do. In return, I will do my utmost to be a mother to your daughter."

"And as my wife?"

She blushed so deeply, she might have been a virgin confronting the prospect of intimacy with a man for the first time, rather than a widow who'd borne a child. "I will honor my vows to the extent that you wish me to."

"In other words, you will be dutiful?"

She looked as if she'd taken a bite out of an apple and found only half a worm left behind in the remainder. "I will do my best. And if you'd like me to sign a prenuptial contract, I'm willing to do that, too."

"Why would I ask such a thing of you?"

"As a token of my good faith. I'm not so mercenary that I'd marry you solely for your money, then seek a divorce as soon as the ink dried on the marriage certificate."

"I'm glad to hear it," he said wryly, "although in all fairness, I must point out that, had you planned to do so, you would most certainly fail. I do not believe in divorce, and those who do strike me as spineless weaklings unwilling to fight for something they presumably once found eminently desirable. I therefore urge you to think very carefully before you sacrifice yourself for your son's sake because, eventually, he will outgrow the need for your protection. Marry me, however, and you will remain my wife as long as we both shall live."

"I understand," she said. "And in the same spirit of full disclosure, I think it only fair to introduce you to my son before you make any further commitment to me."

"He's here?"

"Yes. We had a…trying morning, so I put him down for an afternoon nap, but if I don't wake him soon, I'll have trouble getting him to settle down tonight."

"Then I would very much like to get to know him."

Briefly she held his gaze, and in that moment, he saw the exhausted defeat her eyes could not hide. "Once you do, you might live to regret asking us to share your life."

The boy was in trouble, he realized; and she, at the end of her rope in dealing with him. Stirred to sympathy, because he knew firsthand the pitfalls of single parenthood, he said gently, "If you're trying to warn me off, Corinne, you should know that I never walk away from a challenge."

"You haven't met Matthew," she said, and with a last doubtful glance, she disappeared upstairs.

CHAPTER FOUR

ONCE SAFELY UPSTAIRS, Corinne shut herself in her room and collapsed on the bed, shaking. The shock of finding Raffaello Orsini on her doorstep had robbed her of her faculties. How else could she account for blurting out that she was prepared to marry him?

Agreeing in writing to his proposal had been insanity enough. Going so far as to order a courier to deliver her acceptance, even worse. But always at the back of her mind had been the notion that, before she actually turned the letter over to the messenger, she'd come to her senses. Or Mr. Orsini would come to his, and rescind his offer before any damage was done.

For him to show up out of the blue and leave her with little choice but to tell him her decision to his face was nothing short of emotional blackmail. Nor did it help that her memory hadn't played her false and he was every bit as good-looking as she'd thought on first meeting. No woman could be expected to act rationally when confronted by such a specimen of masculine beauty. Especially not when, as appearances went, hers left much to be desired. Faded blue sweatpants and top, and fuzzy felt slippers hardly showed her at her best. As for her hair, escaping in wild strands from the elastic she'd used to hold it back while she baked a cake…well, if she'd stood in a pail of water and stuffed a steel skewer into the nearest electrical outlet, she couldn't have looked more deranged.

Next door, the sound of Matthew stirring catapulted her off the bed. Shedding the sweatpants, socks and top in record time, she exchanged them for sheer black panty hose, tailored black slacks, a long-sleeved white shirt and flat-heeled black shoes. Yanking her hair free of the elastic, she raked a brush through it until it fell into some sort of reasonable order. One last glance in the mirror told her she looked about as cheerful as a grave digger, so she added a pair of red hoop earrings to the ensemble, a touch of gloss to her lips and a swipe of blusher over her pale cheeks.

Next door, Matthew kicked idly at the wall dividing his room from hers, a sure sign he was growing restless at his confinement. "We have company, sweetie," she told him, as she hastily washed his face and stuffed him into a clean pair of jeans. "Remember your manners, okay?"

Then taking him by the hand, she led him downstairs to meet the man who might become his stepfather.

She found Raffaello Orsini thumbing through the week-end newspaper, but he put it aside at her return. "This is my son," she said. "Say hello to Mr. Orsini, Matthew."

For a moment, she thought he'd balk at the idea, but eventually he peeped out from behind her legs and managed a shy, "Hi."

Raffaello bent down and gravely shook his hand. "*Ciao,* Matthew. It's a pleasure to meet you at last."

Clearly taken with this kind of man-to-man interaction,

Matthew emerged from her protection and offered, "Guess what? I've got a train set."

"Have you?" he replied, looking properly impressed. "Will you show me?"

"Okay."

From her post at the breakfast bar, Corinne watched as the pair of them hauled the various parts out of the toy box, then embarked on a solemn discussion of the best configuration for the railroad tracks. What was it about trains that had grown men and little boys so enraptured, she wondered. Raffaello Orsini's immaculately tailored suit probably cost more than she earned in six months, but he didn't seem to care as he sprawled out on her old rug, engrossed in assembling a plastic bridge while Matthew hooked the engine to a line of carriages.

"How old are you, Matthew?" she heard him ask.

"Four." Matthew stopped what he was doing long enough to hold up four fingers and, to Corinne's horror, went on, "How old are you?"

To his credit, Raffaello didn't so much as blink. "Thirty-five," he said, adjusting a curving length of track to fit under the bridge. "Very old indeed."

Matthew eyed him speculatively. "Are you my new daddy?"

Raffaello spared her an amused glance. "Not quite yet, no."

Dismayed, Corinne realized she should have anticipated something like this. Matthew often asked why he didn't have a daddy like other children they saw at the park, and although she'd explained that Joe had died when Matthew was still a baby, her son had never quite grasped the idea that she couldn't just go out and buy him another.

Blithely unaware of the exchange or the sudden heightened tension in the room, Matthew struck off in a different direction. "I like horses."

"So do I," Raffaello replied, not missing a beat. "Which ones do you like best?"

"Brown ones."

"A very good choice."

"And black ones."

"Big or small?"

"Big."

"Me, too." He offered his palm for a high-five. Matthew burst into a grin and slapped at his hand with four-year-old enthusiasm. And Corinne released the breath she'd been holding, only then acknowledging to herself how relieved she was that the two of them were getting along so famously, not for any other reason than that she so badly wanted someone to see her son in a positive light.

Over Matthew's head, Raffaello glanced her way a second time, his gaze disturbingly intense. "It appears your boy and I have a great deal in common. A cause for celebration, wouldn't you say?"

"I suppose so, yes." Flustered, she hesitated, aware that the next move was up to her. "It's getting a bit late for afternoon tea. Would you...um, care to join us for dinner, instead?"

"I have a better idea." Ruffling Matthew's hair, he hoisted himself to his feet. "Why don't I take us all out for dinner?"

"Oh, I don't think so, thank you. There's not much in

the way of fine dining in this neighborhood, just mostly family places that are child-friendly."

"*I* am child-friendly, Corinne."

So it seemed. But she doubted he'd ever dined in the kind of establishment she had in mind. "I'm talking about a restaurant with high chairs and booster seats, and children's menus and crayons for coloring paper place mats."

"But is it also man-and-woman-friendly?"

"Well, parent-friendly, at any rate."

"Then both you and I also qualify, do we not?"

Was he never at a loss for an answer? "Fine," she said, throwing out her hands in defeat. "Don't say I didn't warn you."

They went to a place just far enough away to warrant riding in the limousine he'd left waiting on the road outside the complex because it was too big to fit in any of the visitor parking stalls. Matthew was in seventh heaven, fascinated by the uniformed driver and luxurious leather built-in child safety seat, and wanted to know everything about the television set and multitude of other gadgets not to be found in her ancient van.

"He is interested in this new experience," Raffaello said, when she apologized for the barrage of questions. "I would find it strange if he was not."

Once seated in the restaurant, she looked around, seeing it as he must. Ketchup bottles, salt and pepper shakers, little packets of sugar and a paper napkin holder, all arranged at one end of a table finished in imitation wood. Plastic-covered menus offering variations on chicken strips, fish and chips and hamburgers. Thick white plates, sturdy enough to withstand clumsy young fingers. Water glasses etched by too many cycles in the dishwasher. Plain stainless steel cutlery. And a motherly server who asked him cheerfully, "What's everyone having tonight, hon?"

Unfazed, he looked inquiringly at Corinne. "Chicken strips for my son, and no sauce, please," she said, mortified by the woman's blithely misplaced familiarity. Couldn't she see he was *different* from everyone else in the place?

"And for you, Corinne?" he inquired.

"I haven't decided," she muttered and made a pretense of studying the menu.

Turning to the server, he said, "What do you recommend, *signora?*"

"The burgers," she replied without hesitation, using her pencil to point out the selection. "Plain, with cheese, mushroom, bacon or any combination of same, all made from scratch, and the best in town."

"Then that's what I'll have. A burger with mushrooms."

"Coffee with that, hon?"

He nodded, causing the overhead light to glint in his dark hair. *"Si, per favore."*

"That's Italian, right? I recognize it from that old Marlon Brando movie, *The Godfather.*" She let out a wheeze of laughter and dug him in the ribs. "Not part of the Mafia, are you, hon?"

"Not that I know of," he said, his grin dazzling enough to light up the night.

"I'll have the same as my friend," Corinne interjected, dying inside. "And a small glass of apple juice for my son."

Until their food arrived—which didn't take long, thank goodness—Raffaello entertained Matthew by helping him color his paper place mat, and engaged Corinne in small talk. Not that she contributed much to the conversation; she was still too rattled.

This was not how she'd foreseen the evening turning out, although she supposed it could have been worse. Matthew was happy enough to divide his time between scribbling in red crayon all over his place mat and devouring his chicken strips. And despite her misgivings, Raffaello seemed perfectly at ease, as if sitting in a vinyl-upholstered booth and dining on a lowly hamburger were normal everyday occurrences for him. From her perspective, however, the scene was too surreal to pass for anything even approaching normal.

What was a sophisticated Italian megamogul in an exquisite custom-tailored suit doing, dipping French fries in ketchup, and apparently enjoying the experience? What was *she* doing, entertaining thoughts of marrying him? And how long before Matthew tired of being on his best behavior and started acting up? Already he was squirming in his seat and asking to be allowed to leave the table.

Noticing, Raffaello said, "He has had enough of this place."

"I'm afraid so, yes."

"Then since we are also finished eating, we will leave."

In short order, he had summoned their server, paid the bill and ushered them through the rain to the waiting limousine. "This weather," he growled, handing her into the warmth and comfort of the car, "is uncivilized."

You probably think we are, too, she almost answered, as Matthew voiced a noisy objection at not being allowed to crawl over to the pane of glass separating driver from passengers, and plant his sticky fingers all over it. "I'm so sorry, Raffaello," she muttered, finally managing to buckle the little rebel into the safety seat.

Raffaello, though, appeared undisturbed and waved aside her apology. "Relax, Corinne. There is no harm done."

"I can't relax," she admitted. "I want you to like him."

"What is there not to like? He has a boy's natural curiosity for the world around him. I would be disturbed if he had not."

But his actions when they reached the town house complex belied his words. Although he escorted them to their front door and even went so far as to carry Matthew, who obstinately refused to walk the short distance, he refused her offer to come inside and sample the cake. "*Grazie,* but no," he said. "I have much to do before returning to Sicilia." And after brushing a kiss on each of her cheeks, he hurried away through the cold wet night as if he couldn't be gone fast enough.

So where does that leave us, she wondered, staring after him, confused. Was the marriage arrangement on, or off? Had she failed some unspoken test? Shown herself to be unsuitable substitute wife and surrogate mother material, after all?

He did not contact her the next day, nor the day after that. Not sure whether she was insulted or relieved, Corinne did her best to put him out of her mind as thoroughly as he appeared to have put her out of his. Viewed rationally, the whole marriage idea had been doomed from the outset. She was lucky he'd recognized that before they took matters to the next level. And if she experienced a certain disappointment at the outcome, it had to do more with the spark of attraction she'd felt for him than it had with any real regret.

It had been such a long time since a man had piqued her interest. Too long, apparently. Why else was she finding it so hard to dismiss him from her thoughts?

Then, when she'd almost reconciled herself to never seeing him again, he blew back into her life on the tail end of a late January gale. At least on this occasion, he warned her ahead of time with a phone call, so that she was prepared when he actually arrived at her door, quite late in the evening, three days after his first visit.

"*Ciao,* again," he said, filling her tiny front entrance hall with his windswept presence, and again dusting her cheeks with a cool kiss. "I brought this for later."

"This" was a bottle of Krug, kept properly chilled in a wine saver.

"Why?"

"To seal our contract and celebrate our forthcoming marriage."

Somehow containing the annoying bubble of delight suddenly exploding inside her, she said, "I thought you'd backed out on the deal. Had second thoughts and returned to Sicily."

"Without you and your son?" He appeared perplexed. Amazed even, as though someone present must be a fool and since he wasn't it, that left only her. "Had we not reached an agreement?"

"Yes, but—"

"Then why would you assume I'd changed my mind?"

"Probably because of the way you left things up in the air after your last visit. The way you took off, claiming you had business to take care of, gave me the impression we were no longer part of your plans."

"I have been occupied having a lawyer draw up the terms of our agreement, and arranging for you to be properly welcomed to my home."

Her elation dwindled away as swiftly as it had arisen. "So you've decided to protect yourself with a prenuptial contract, after all."

"No." Following her into the family room, he withdrew a legal-looking document from his inside pocket and slapped it down on the breakfast bar. "I decided I must protect you and your son, in the event that you should find yourself a widow a second time. Take a look for yourself, if you don't believe me."

Swallowing, she said, "I see."

"I hope you do, Corinne." He fixed her in a very direct, smoky-gray gaze. "Ours might not be a conventional marriage by most standards, but it nonetheless requires a mutual investment of trust if it is to succeed. I am not a man to break my word. You may rely on that, no matter what else you might find lacking in me."

His calm logic, the straightforward manner in which he spoke to her, left her feeling both foolish and ashamed. Not everyone was as irresponsible and glib with the truth as her late husband. "I do believe you, Raffaello," she said. "And from everything Lindsay told me about you, I also know I can trust you. I wouldn't contemplate putting Matthew's future in your hands, if I didn't. It's just that, when it comes to him, I'm…fragile. I want what is best for him."

"That is the way of all good mothers."

"I'd like to think so, but lately, I haven't been doing too well in that department. The night we met, though, you said that our children are the innocents and deserved the best we could give them, and the more I thought about it, the more I realized you were right. It's not the only reason I changed my mind about our joining forces, but it's the one that made the deepest impression."

"So why the sudden loss of faith in me?"

"Because when my husband was killed and I found myself a single mother with a baby, I promised myself I was done with relying on other people because the only person I could ever really depend on was myself. I made up my mind that, from there on, it would be just me and my child, and I'd never do anything to jeopardize his happiness or security. Then you came along and almost overnight I decided to throw in my lot with you. But after what seemed to be a promising beginning, two days went by without a word from you, and it struck me how close I might have come to breaking that promise and putting Matthew's future at risk."

"I'm sorry if I caused you unnecessary worry. It was not my intention." He crossed the room to where she stood by the fireplace, and took her hands firmly in his. "Whatever the future holds, I give you my solemn word, neither you nor your boy will suffer as a result of this marriage."

His hands were cold, yet his touch filled her with a subtle warmth. She couldn't recall the last time she'd felt so safe.

"And I'll do my best to see that you never regret making that promise."

"Then we have a deal?"

"We have a deal."

She expected he'd release her then and open the wine, but he didn't. Still holding her hands, he drew her closer and for the first time, placed his mouth on hers in a kiss so fleeting, she wondered if she'd imagined it. But the bolt of heat, streaking to some near-forgotten area below her waist, assured her otherwise.

Shaken, she pulled away and said, "So what's next?"

"For now," he said, the amusement rippling in his voice leaving her aghast at how he might have interpreted her question, "I suggest you read the contract. Then, if it meets with your approval, we'll both sign it and toast to our joint venture with a glass of champagne."

"I don't need to read it. I already told you, I trust you."

"I can't possibly agree to that. Under no circumstances should you ever sign anything, let alone a legal document, without first reading it." He inclined his head to where the contract lay on the breakfast bar. "Go ahead, Corinne. It's brief and to the point and I doubt you'll have any difficulty understanding it, but if you do have any concerns, now's the time to air them."

He was quite right, of course, on all points. Just because he stirred various other body parts to outrageous response was no excuse for her brain to turn to mush. And the contract, all of two pages long, couldn't have been more plainly set out.

She agreed to live with him in Sicily as soon as possible, once the agreement was signed.

They would share parenting responsibility for his daughter and her son.

Should Raffaello predecease her, she would inherit half his estate, the other half being left to Elisabetta. Should Corinne predecease Raffaello, Matthew would inherit her share of the estate.

Should either parent die before the children reached the

age of majority, the remaining parent would undertake to care for both minors in the manner to which they had become accustomed.

Should both parents die before the children achieved the age of majority, the estate would be held in trust and a guardian, to be decided upon mutually by both parties, would be appointed to administer the funds and assume legal custody of the children.

"Well?" he inquired, as she finished reading.

"I'm overwhelmed by your generosity. If I have any reservations at all, it's that I'm not bringing enough to the bargain."

"You are fulfilling my wife's last wishes. That is enough to satisfy me."

My wife, he said, and Corinne's spirits sagged a little at that. *What will he call me, once we're married?* she wondered, signing her name next to his in the space provided at the bottom of the contract. *My substitute spouse? My wife's stand-in?*

"Now that business is taken care of, we can celebrate," he declared, stripping the foil away from the bottle of Krug. "Where do you keep your champagne flutes, Corinne?"

Fortunately she had a couple, though they were neither very fine nor very elegant, but if he noticed, he was kind enough not to comment. Instead he tapped the rim of his against hers and said, "To the future!"

"And to our children. They are, after all, what this is really all about." She ushered him to the couch next to the fireplace. "So what comes next?"

"Tomorrow, I shall obtain a marriage license. The wedding will take place as soon as it can be arranged, but most certainly within the week."

"Don't be ridiculous!" she exclaimed, startled enough to forget about being polite. "A week won't leave me nearly enough time! I have to close my business, pack, speak to my landlord—"

"Mere details, Corinne. Now that you've made your decision, all that remains is for you to decide which items you wish to take with you to Sicily. I will see to the rest."

"But—"

"And you understand, I'm sure, that I prefer not to be away from Elisabetta any longer than is absolutely necessary."

"I do, of course." She lifted her shoulders helplessly, knowing that if the situation were reversed, she'd be hopping with impatience to get back to Matthew. Still, what he proposed struck her as virtually impossible to achieve in a matter of days.

Correctly reading her doubts, he touched her cheek briefly. "Trust me, *cara mia.*"

"I do," she said, and was surprised to realize that it was the truth. "I'm just not used to being taken care of, that's all."

"Get used to it. It will be my wedding gift to you." He fixed her in a smiling glance. "You're frowning. Do you doubt my word?"

"No. I just realized something we've overlooked. Matthew should be starting school in September, but he won't be able to do that in Sicily. He doesn't speak the language."

"You worry for nothing, my dear. Elisabetta has a governess who teaches in English as well as Italian. Matthew will fit in very well, and be fluent in Italian by Christmas.

Now, is there any other problem you can think of to delay our wedding?"

"No," she said. "Not a thing."

Events moved quickly after that because, as Corinne quickly learned, Raffaello was not a man to let obstacles stand in his way. In short order, he dealt with her landlord, settled her debts, sent a two-man crew to pack her and Matthew's possessions—mostly photograph albums, toys and a few other treasured mementoes—and arranged for ownership of her catering company to be transferred to three women who'd worked for her occasionally and who, upon hearing she was closing her business, leaped at the chance to run it themselves and bought all her supplies and equipment. The only miracle he didn't pull off was securing passports for her and Matthew, and that was only because she'd already obtained them herself, two years previously, when she'd won a trip to Mexico.

Consequently, exactly ten days after meeting him, she stood before a marriage commissioner in downtown Vancouver, at twenty after ten in the morning, and became Mrs. Raffaello Orsini. At a quarter to three that same afternoon, accompanied by her new husband and her son, she boarded an Air Canada jet bound for Rome and, half an hour later, found herself on the first leg of the journey to her new life.

CHAPTER FIVE

THE PHOTOGRAPHS of his home didn't begin to do justice to the place. Villa di Cascata was, quite simply, breathtaking. Vast, luxurious, it could have passed for a royal residence, and considering the style in which she'd traveled to reach it, Corinne shouldn't have been surprised. First class passage to Rome, followed by corporate jet to a private landing strip carved out of the Sicilian countryside ought to have warned her she was setting foot in a world far removed from what she was used to.

As if to underscore the fact, the message was driven home with a vengeance, the second Raffaello introduced her to his mother and aunt. The last word in dignified elegance, Malvolia Orsini and Leonora Pacenzia stood side by side in the grand entrance hall, their dark eyes wary as they sized up the stranger suddenly thrust into their midst.

"Welcome," and "We are pleased to meet you," they said, their English almost as flawless as Raffaello's. But the words lacked any real warmth, and in all fairness, who could blame them if they thought she was nothing but a fortune hunter, when Corinne had leveled the same accusation at herself a hundred times or more in the last week?

Beside them, she felt inadequate, unsophisticated, her wedding outfit, a pretty dove-gray suit, which had seemed such a good buy two days ago, sadly lacking beside the understated elegance of her mother-in-law's black dress. The woman's nostrils practically twitched with distaste as she surveyed Corinne's skirt where Matthew's sticky fingers had left their mark.

You try keeping stain and wrinkle-free after almost fifteen hours in a confined space with a four-year-old, Corinne thought resentfully.

Finally tearing her gaze away from the offending sight, Malvolia switched her attention to Matthew. "And this, of course must be—?"

"My son," Corinne said, unable to quell her confrontational tone. She wouldn't be responsible for her actions if the woman showed even a smidgeon of disapproval for Matthew.

Whatever her opinion of her son's new wife, however, Malvolia Orsini's response to Matthew couldn't be faulted. Bending her aristocratic spine until she was at eye level with him and holding out her arms, she crooned, "*Ciao,* little one. What a handsome boy you are. Will you come here and tell me your name?"

Wretched traitor that he was, he walked unhesitatingly into her embrace and said, "Matthew. What's yours?"

"I am Signora Orsini."

"Are you my new baby-sitter?"

"No," she said, stroking the hair away from his forehead. "I am your new grandmother, but you may call me Nonna." Then straightening, she beckoned to her sister. "And this is your new aunt, Zia Leonora."

The sister, a slightly less intimidating woman, gave

him a hug, and shot Corinne a glance. "You have a fine son, *signora.*"

"I agree," Corinne said.

"And somewhere in these parts, I have a fine daughter," Raffaello remarked to his mother, slipping a casual arm around Corinne's waist. "How is it that she's not here to meet her new stepbrother?"

"I sent her to the stables with Lucinda. Lorenzo promised to give her a riding lesson."

"Why now, *Madre mia?* You knew when to expect us and surely must be aware how anxious I am to see her and introduce her to our new family members."

Malvolia stiffened imperceptibly. "It was better, I decided, not to overwhelm your...wife with too much, too soon." She laid just enough emphasis on *wife* to make it plain that she in no way considered Corinne to be anything other than an upstart who had no business using the villa's front door, when there was a perfectly good one at the back designed expressly for servants. "She would prefer to freshen up before meeting Elisabetta, would you not, *signora?*"

"Thank you," Corinne returned with equal formality, "I would. Very much."

"A wise decision." Malvolia inclined her head in regal acknowledgment before delivering a final barb. "You have only one chance to make a good first impression, after all."

The subtle insult almost undid Corinne. She'd learned long ago that tears brought nothing but puffy eyes and a red nose, and that the only way to overcome obstacles was to fight them. But at that moment, she had no fight left in her. It was now Saturday and she hadn't slept a wink since Thursday night. Not only that, despite the drawbacks inherent in her old life, cutting all ties with it had turned out to be a lot harder than she'd expected. The town house might not have amounted to much, especially by Malvolia Orsini's exalted standards, but it had been home, whereas this place...

Choking back another threatened meltdown, Corinne took stock of her surroundings. A circular staircase rose in a sweeping curve beneath a high domed ceiling whose stained-glass panes bathed the creamy marble steps in muted rose and mauve, and touched the ornate black iron bannister with gold. Illuminated wall niches displayed various objets d'art: a bronze life-size hawk, wings spread, alighting on a tree branch; an alabaster bust of Napoleon; a priceless Ming vase.

Although indisputably magnificent, the place was foreign territory, and she very much the alien. She couldn't imagine there'd ever come a time when she'd feel comfortable with such grandeur.

Leonora must have seen how close she'd come to losing her composure because she said quite kindly, "*Venite, signora,* and I will show you the way to your suite of rooms."

"Do so, and I will keep this little one amused." Malvolia placed a propriety hand on Matthew's head. "He will be quite happy with me, *signora.*"

At any other time, Corinne might have disputed that, but right then, escaping her mother-in-law's cool, assessing gaze was uppermost in her mind, and she seized on the aunt's invitation with the desperation of a drowning woman clutching a life ring.

Watching them leave, Raffaello noted Corinne's stiff posture, the square set of her slender shoulders, the jerky, marionettelike motion of her legs as she climbed the stairs. He'd witnessed much the same taut apprehension throughout the long flight from Canada, half a world away. Although her son had curled up next to her, a stuffed toy dog she'd taken from his backpack tucked next to his cheek, and slept soundly for eight hours straight, not once in all that time had she relaxed. Instead she'd remained bolt upright in her seat, her gaze empty and every fragile bone strung to its neighbor with tension wire.

Her gaze wasn't empty now, though. As she turned to follow Leonora, he caught the utter desolation in her eyes, and he knew who'd put it there.

Calling on one of the household staff to keep an eye on Matthew, Raffaello waited until they were alone then grasped his mother's elbow and steered her firmly through the anteroom beyond the hall, and into the *soggiorno*. "I hoped this wouldn't be necessary, and that enough time had passed for you to come to terms with my new living arrangements, Mother, but since you clearly have not, we are going to arrive at an understanding of how you treat my family. You might disapprove—"

"Of course I disapprove!" she exclaimed, shaking her arm free. "Your informing us you planned to fly halfway around the world to persuade a woman you've never met to become your wife and a stepmother to your daughter, was shocking enough. But I told myself you acted on the spur of the moment, driven by your lasting devotion to Lindsay, and that you'd come to your senses before any real damage was done."

"Then you underestimated my determination, as you very well knew when I phoned to tell you the wedding was a fait accompli."

"You think confronting me now with this woman—this foreigner who has no more knowledge or understanding than a flea of our way of life—is enough to persuade me you have done the right thing?"

"This *foreigner* you dismiss so contemptuously happens to be my wife, Mother."

"Is that what you call her?" she retaliated. "After little more than a week of shopping, I'd have thought 'souvenir' a more appropriate description."

"Then I suggest you modify your thinking," he said, not even trying to hide his displeasure, "because like it or not, Corinne is here to stay and I will not tolerate your treating her with disrespect."

His mother sniffed disparagingly. "You'll be telling me next that this is a love match."

"Not in the least. It is an arrangement arrived at solely for the benefit of our children."

"And her. Or are you going to pretend she is a woman of independent means, and was not in the least swayed by your wealth and position?"

"No. I'm going to remind you that you took much the same exception to Lindsay when I first brought her here as my wife. Yet, at the end, you mourned her death as deeply as anyone."

"Lindsay adored you, and you, her. She bore you a child, gave me a granddaughter. What is this new wife bringing to the table beyond an appetite for comfort and financial security?"

"That is between me and her."

Malvolia sank into her favorite chair near the fireplace. "If finding a woman to give you comfort mattered so much,

Raffaello, I can name at least a dozen here in Sicily who'd have been more than happy to call themselves Signora Orsini. Women of breeding and background, who'd have shared our customs and language. Instead you come with a stranger. What makes her so special?"

"She shares a knowledge and love of Lindsay, and will be a good mother to Elisabetta."

At that, his mother uttered a yelp of outrage mixed with distress. "And what of me and your aunt? Where do we fit into this new regime? Or have we outlived our usefulness and must now be banished to the dowager house next door?"

"I would resort to such an extreme measure with the utmost reluctance," he said, fixing her in a telling glance. "You are, and always will be Elisabetta's cherished grandmother and Leonora her great-aunt. I'd even go so far as to say that Corinne hopes you'll both eventually find room in your big and loving hearts for her son."

His mother's expression softened at the mention of Matthew. "He is an engaging little thing, that I do admit. So fearless and forthright in the way he looks one in the eye. And I admit it will be good for Elisabetta to have a playmate closer to her own age. I sometimes think she spends too much time with old women."

"Then we understand one another?"

She sighed. "Yes. And I apologize for my earlier remarks. I was too harsh and am, perhaps, too quick to find fault. But I am afraid for you, my son. Granted, this woman seems respectable enough, but how much do you really know of her?"

"As much as I need to know, and I'd have thought you knew *me* well enough to trust my judgment, and that I could count on your support now."

"You can, Raffaello. I am on your side always." She sighed again. "Which means that, ultimately, I'm on hers, too."

"Thank you for that." He dropped a kiss on her cheek and left, anxious to find Corinne and do what he could to reassure her. Theirs might not be a match made in heaven, but nor had it been forged in hell.

He found her standing in the middle of the sitting room in their suite, her face a study in dismay. Joining her, he cupped her jaw and gently tilted her chin so that her gaze met his. "What is it, Corinne?"

"I'm trying to figure out what I'm doing here."

"Where else would you be, *cara mia?* This is your new home."

"No, Raffaello," she said, her eyes glassy with unshed tears. "It's *your* home, but it'll never be mine."

"If you're referring to my mother's less than gracious reception—"

"She was merely stating the obvious, which is that I don't belong here."

"Certainly you do. You are my wife."

"Label me anything you please, but it won't change the fact that I'm as much out of place here as a weed in a rose garden."

"That is not so. I see you as a vital link between the past and the future. Remember, this isn't about you and me, and certainly not about my mother or aunt. We married because of Matthew and Elisabetta."

As if to drive home his point, the faint sound of children's laughter drifted up from the garden. "Who've obviously met and hit it off famously," he added, and taking her by the hand, he opened the French doors at one end of the sitting room and led her to the wide veranda that ran the width of the upper floor of the house.

At the foot of the sloping lawn directly below, the children played with one of the puppies from the litter born ten weeks ago in the stables. Although the sky was clear, the temperature hovered around eight degrees Celsius, but they didn't feel the cold. They were too busy having a good time to notice it was still early February which, even in Sicily, meant that winter wasn't quite over yet.

"You see, Corinne? Already they have become friends. Look at your son, then tell me again that you made a mistake in bringing him here."

She leaned against the iron railing, some of the strain easing from her face as she watched the boy tumbling around on the lawn. He was much like a puppy himself, all high spirits and boundless energy. "I haven't heard him laugh like that in a very long time," she admitted softly.

"Surely that is enough to relieve your doubts? Or am I so repulsive to you as a husband that nothing can make you glad you agreed to our marriage?"

She raised startled eyes to his. "It's not you, Raffaello, it's me. Dress it up any way you like, but there's no question in anyone's mind that, of the two of us, I made the better bargain."

"You're speaking of material advantages, but—"

"Well, yes," she said, with a rueful laugh. "Look around you, for heaven's sake! Both floors of my old town house would fit inside this suite, and still leave room to spare." With a sweeping motion of her arm, she gestured to the chairs and couches in the sitting room; the occasional tables, the writing desk, the lamps, the paintings. Fine quality accessories which, in his world, hardly merited notice. "And never mind the small matter of marble floors and exotic furnishings and priceless art. You've introduced me to a level of luxury beyond anything I knew existed."

"I never made a secret of the fact that I have money, Corinne."

"You didn't spell out exactly how much, either."

"You didn't ask."

She let out a shocked exclamation. "I would never be so crass as to do that!"

"Precisely," he said. "You accepted me on trust, as I accepted you. You can't put a price ticket on that. So let there be no more talk of wealth or assets. They play no part in the equation which brought us to this point, so put them out of your mind and let me introduce you to your new stepdaughter."

After a moment's hesitation, she nodded. "All right, I'd like that. But your mother was right. I need to make myself presentable first—and by the way, thank you."

"For what?"

"Taking the time to make me feel better. Reminding me why we got married yesterday." She offered a brave, tentative smile. "For being you."

She undid him with that smile. Drawing her to him, he said, "Not much about yesterday followed tradition. There was no wedding cake, no first dance, no champagne, nor did I carry you over the threshold of your new home, but this much at least I can do."

And he bent his head to kiss her. Not deeply, or at length, not urgently, or with fire, but simply as a token to

seal their union and let her know she could count on him
to stand by her.

What he had *not* counted on was the impact of her body
imprinted against his. The response it aroused in him shook
him to the core. What he'd intended to be tame turned feral. Primitive. Hot and hungry and deeply sensual.

He was no saint. His sex drive hadn't died with Lindsay.
He'd known physical need and desire in the years since she'd
been gone, and he'd satisfied both with women who asked
nothing of him but a night of mutual pleasure. But they never
touched him, not in any real sense. Not in his heart or his soul.
They didn't arouse his tenderness or the urge to protect them.
Their memory didn't stay with him. By the time he left them,
he'd sometimes forgotten their names, which was quite fine
with them. They were experienced enough to know how the
game was played. To know the score.

Kissing Corinne shouldn't have been all that much different. Ideally they should both have enjoyed the moment.
Perhaps used it as a stepping stone to greater intimacy.
They were, after all, husband and wife, and he had no interest in breaking his marriage vows and straying to another
woman's bed. But she should not have engaged his heart
with her fragility and vulnerability. Even if his body responded with unbridled enthusiasm, his mind should not
have grown cloudy with emotion. Theirs was not that kind
of marriage.

On the last point, she obviously agreed with him, although her response was more explosive than his, and for
reasons a lot less flattering. Choking back a sob, she planted
her palms flat against his chest, and pushed him away. "What
was that?" she cried thickly, tears streaming down her face.

"An error of judgment, and my fault entirely," he said bleakly. "It meant nothing and was in no way a betrayal of the people we once were married to. You have no reason to feel guilty."

She stared at him, her blue eyes bruised with shock and pain.

"Forget it, Corinne," he urged, taking a linen handkerchief from his breast pocket and drying her tears. "Go about your business as if it never happened. You said something earlier about freshening up before you meet Elisabetta."

"So I did." She stared around the room, her eyes dazed and unfocussed. "Where can I wash my face?"

Don't you mean, rinse out your mouth to rid yourself of the taste of me? he almost said, but there was awkwardness enough between them, without his making matters any worse. "The bathrooms are through there." He pointed out the door on the other side of the small foyer. "Yours is the one on the left. Why don't you enjoy a leisurely bath, then take a nap? You'll have plenty of time to dress for dinner later. We usually meet for cocktails at half-past seven."

"But what about Matthew?"

"Right now, Matthew is in good hands and having too much fun to miss you." Turning her around, he propelled her gently across the room, opened the door to the bedroom end of the suite and steered her through. "You've had an exhausting few days, Corinne. Do yourself a favor and let someone else take over for once. There'll be time enough in the weeks to come, to establish some sort of routine with the children. For the next hour or two, forget everything else and concentrate on you."

* * *

She didn't think it possible. How could any woman concentrate, when her entire world had tilted on its axis in a matter of seconds?

Raffaello might have been gallant enough to take the blame for what had happened between them, but it hadn't been his fault at all. It had been hers, albeit by accident, and while he might be able to forget it, she never would.

Apart from the night they'd signed their marriage agreement and immediately after the wedding ceremony, he'd only ever kissed her on each cheek, in the way that Europeans did. So when he went to kiss her again before leaving her to take her bath, she anticipated it would be more of the same, and lifted her face, angling it toward him just so.

The trouble was, her timing was off and without her knowing quite how it happened, her mouth had blundered against his, briefly and clumsily. But just as a spark could ignite a can of gasoline and turn it into a raging inferno, so it had been with them at that moment.

Their lips clung, fused. The breath locked in her throat, searing her lungs with its heat. Stunned, she swayed against him. His mouth was the stuff women's fantasies were made of. Masterfully seductive; persuasively erotic.

His hands slid from her shoulders to her waist and he pressed her closer. Tightened his hold, trapping her clenched fist between their bodies, against the firm, warm contours of his chest. And what had begun awkwardly transposed itself into something wonderful and unforgettable.

His mouth had lingered. One hand strayed to the curve of her hip and exerted just the slightest pressure. Aware that he'd grown hard against her, she'd felt a shifting inside, as if her body—her feminine, female parts—were awakening from a long winter's sleep and preparing to bask in summer's heat again.

She'd found the sensation at once so powerful and exquisite that her eyes had filled with tears at the miracle of it. A terrible thudding hunger had overtaken her, and she'd ached for him so badly that she'd had to push him away, or risk embarrassing them both by begging him to make love to her.

In a perfect world, that might not have been such a bad thing, but in reality, she knew in his heart, he'd been kissing Lindsay, and had attributed a similarly misplaced response to herself, assuming she'd been thinking of Joe. Why else had he said she had no reason to feel guilty?

But what would he say if she told him he'd been mistaken, and that she'd known very well what she was doing and whose arms were wrapped around her?

What would he think if she confessed that the early passion between her and Joe had soon burned itself out, and left behind a residue of disillusionment, obligation and resentment so bitter, she'd actually felt more relief than sorrow when he was killed?

Would Raffaello then relegate her to the ranks of those he'd so scathingly dismisssed as being too spineless to fix a marriage gone wrong? Decide he'd acted too hastily and settled for someone not nearly good enough to fill Lindsay's hallowed shoes?

She'd burned too many bridges to risk finding out, and so she'd seized on his suggestion that she take extra time for herself, and escaped before she said something she'd regret.

Her bathroom, connected to his by a mirrored dressing

room, was enormous, with a curved window looking out onto a tiny private garden with orchids growing in the niches of an old stone wall, and a miniature waterfall cascading into a black marble bowl. The extensive use of pink-veined ivory marble inside, the array of toiletries set out on the vanity, the thick, velvety bath towels, deep claw-foot tub and glass-enclosed steam shower again all seemed to point to the fact that she was so far out of her element here that, even without her shameful secret, she'd never measure up.

"Oh, snap out of it!" she berated herself, letting the rush of water filling the tub drown out the self-pitying voice whining in her head. "You're here for the children, not the man and definitely not for yourself. And if that means putting up with a suspicious mother-in-law and more luxury than you ever guessed existed under one roof, at least it beats not knowing where next month's rent's coming from. Earn your keep, do well what you've been hired to do and don't ask for the moon on top of it all."

Stripping away her clothes, she sank up to her neck in the warm, scented water and soaked away the ache and dust of travel. Then she climbed into the marriage bed and fell asleep.

When she awoke, darkness had fallen and the ormolu clock on the bedside table showed ten after six. Time to get ready to face her husband again, not to mention his dragon of a mother.

And yet, she thought as she dressed, how fair was she to condemn the woman for reservations she herself would certainly have entertained if Matthew showed up with a complete stranger and introduced her as his wife?

Checking herself one last time in the dressing room mirror, she felt reasonably pleased with what she saw. Her hair gleamed from its recent shampooing, a shimmer of blusher lent color to her pale cheeks, and a touch of concealer disguised the dark shadows under her eyes. As for what she was wearing, if the best she could manage was the black dress, black pumps and fake pearls she'd worn to her first dinner with Raffaello, at least they were presentable.

Reminding herself it was easier to catch flies with honey rather than vinegar, she pinned a smile on her face and went down to face the evening ahead.

CHAPTER SIX

GASTONE, THE BUTLER, whom she later learned was married to Filomena, the cook, met her at the foot of the stairs and directed her to what he called the *soggiorno*. Loosely translated, it meant sitting room, but to Corinne, hovering unnoticed on the threshold, so pedestrian a description hardly fit the elegant scene before her.

Silk-shaded table lamps offset the ink-black night pressing against the tall, curved windows lining one wall. Those set at right angles next to it opened onto a pillared porch which must, during the day, provide lovely views over the coast.

The furniture was classic Italian Provincial, all clean, pure lines enhanced by sublime brocade upholstery. A white grand piano stood in a curved alcove. Deep, intricate moldings framed the arched entrance and windows. Logs burned in the marble fireplace. Jewel-toned paintings graced the walls. Again, Lindsay's kind of room, as tastefully charming as she herself had been. And set squarely in the middle of it all, Matthew, showing terrifying interest in the carved figure of a horse displayed on a glass-topped table.

"Honey, don't touch—" Corinne exclaimed, darting toward him.

Malvolia, imposing in crushed velvet the color of garnets, paused in the act of sipping from an exquisite Waterford sherry glass. "Ah, here you are at last, Corinna. I was beginning to wonder if you were lost."

You wish, Corinne thought, removing Matthew from the site of potential disaster and parking his wriggling little body next to hers on a couch. He was all spruced up in a clean white shirt and black corduroy pants, she noticed, and didn't appear to have missed her at all. "I'm sorry if I've kept you waiting."

"You haven't. My sister and I are enjoying our cocktail hour, as usual."

Nodding her thanks, Corinne accepted a glass of sherry from the butler and took a firmer grip on her squirming son who was bent on returning to the horse. "I thought Raffaello would be here, too."

"He's spending a little quality time with his daughter. She missed him when he was gone. But they'll join us shortly. Let the child go, Corinna. He's up to no harm."

The name's Corinne, and you have no idea how quickly he could turn this room into a disaster zone, she thought, pasting a stiff smile on her face. "He will be, if he knocks over that statue. It'll smash your glass table."

"The Chinese sculpture, you mean?" Malvolia chirped with amusement. "There's no chance of that, dear girl. It's carved from solid jade, and far too heavy for him to move."

"Nevertheless, I'll feel better if he leaves it alone."

"And I insist that you not worry and let the child be."

It was as well that Raffaello showed up just then, or she might have forgotten herself so far as to lean forward and pinch the woman. As it was, he looked so divinely hand-

some in a silver-gray suit that it was all Corinne could do
to tear her glance away from him and concentrate on the
girl at his side.

Even though Corinne had seen a photograph and thought
herself prepared, Elisabetta in the flesh brought Lindsay
alive again in such startling miniature that Corinne choked
up at the sight of her.

"You're looking more rested, Corinne," Raffaello
remarked, nothing in his manner suggesting he was in any
way referring to their encounter in the bedroom.

Pulling herself together, she said, "I'm feeling much
better, and so glad to meet your daughter at last. Hello,
Elisabetta. I'm Matthew's mommy."

"You're Papa's new wife, as well," the child replied,
with disquieting candor. "Nonna told me all about you."

"Which wasn't very much, *tesoro,*" Malvolia amended,
shooting a nervous glance at Raffaello. "What could I say,
after all, when I myself know almost nothing?"

But the mixture of apprehension and confusion in the
little girl's eyes said plainly enough that finding herself
saddled with a stepmother she hadn't asked for was difficult enough, without anything her grandmother might or
might not have seen fit to add.

"It hardly matters," Corinne said, smiling at the poor
little thing. "Now that I'm here, you can learn all about me
for yourself."

Elisabetta, though, decided getting to know more about
Matthew was a better idea. "Come here," she ordered,
crooking an imperious little finger. "Papa brought home a
new floor puzzle for me, and he's going to help us put it
together, aren't you, Papa?"

"I'll help you get started," he said.

Not needing a second invitation, Matthew charged off to join them. Corinne was just as glad to see him go. Raffaello wouldn't let him run wild, and tomorrow, in private, was soon enough for her to start building a relationship with her self-possessed little stepdaughter. The only immediate drawback was that it now left Corinne at her mother-in-law's inquisitive mercy.

"This is your first visit to Sicily, I understand?" Malvolia said, fixing her in a gimlet-eyed stare.

"Yes. My first visit to Italy, in fact."

"You have not traveled extensively?"

"Not in Europe, no."

"Where were you educated?"

"Mostly in Canada, at the Art Institute of Vancouver, although I did spend three months serving an apprenticeship in New York."

"You are an artist?"

"Of sorts, yes. I studied culinary arts."

"Then you're a cook—or, I suppose, more accurately a chef. How did you manage to juggle such a demanding career with motherhood?"

"It hasn't always been easy."

"I'm sure not." Malvolia regarded her intently a moment. "Raffaello earned his degree in economics in Milano, and a second degree in equine sciences at Colorado State University in America."

"Really? I didn't know he was interested in horses."

"My dear, I suspect you have a great deal to learn about my son. His interest in horse breeding is but one of his passions. But tell us more about your family,

Corinna. Doesn't it upset your parents, to be separated from their grandson?"

"No," she said absently, paying more attention to the trio working on the floor puzzle near the piano, than the woman sitting across from her. Elisabetta was busily fitting pieces of the puzzle together, but Matthew wilted visibly against Raffaello's knee, his lashes drooping as the excitement of the day finally caught up with him.

Then, belatedly aware of the thundering silence her reply had created, Corinne dragged her attention back to the women staring at her in open dismay. "What I mean is, they live in Arizona and barely know him."

"Then you are not close," Malvolia pursued, "in the way that families usually are, that is?"

"No," Corinne said baldly. Why bother pretending, when the truth was bound to come out, sooner or later? "My parents never wanted children. I was an unexpected and unwelcome midlife baby. They were glad when I grew old enough to look out for myself, and showed absolutely no interest in being grandparents."

To give her her due, Malvolia looked quite stricken. "How very sad for you, Corinna. I cannot imagine such a situation. Can you, Leonora?"

"Not at all." Leonora turned pitying eyes on Corinne. "We have always been a close-knit family. And now that you're married to Raffaello, we hope you'll feel part of it, *cara*. You and your son both."

"I hope so, too," she said, "but speaking of my son, he's practically falling asleep on his feet. Is it possible for me to give him his dinner early, and put him to bed before the rest of us sit down to eat?"

"He's already eaten, child," Malvolia said, her tone warmer than it had been hitherto. "Over an hour ago. We don't expect him or Elisabetta to sit through a late adult meal when they're still both so young. As for seeing him to bed, his nanny will do that."

"Nanny?"

"Lucinda. I'd forgotten you've yet to meet her, but you need have no worries. She's been with us since Elisabetta was born, and is very good with children."

"I'm sure she is, but I prefer to take care of him myself, especially tonight. He will be in a strange bed, after all, and he is only four."

After a pause, Malvolia nodded. "You're quite right. We'll hold dinner until he's asleep and you feel comfortable leaving him. I'll have Lucinda show you to the nursery wing."

Overhearing, Raffaello scooped Matthew into his arms and climbed to his feet. "I'll do that. It's time both children went down for the night anyway, and I haven't read my daughter a bedtime story in nearly two weeks. Come on, Elisabetta. You go first and show Corinne which room is Matthew's."

The nursery wing—a term which initially struck horror in Corinne with its Victorian connotations of grim-faced nannies and barred windows—turned out to be three adjoining rooms directly across the hall from the master suite. Already, Matthew's collection of plastic boats were lined up next to the tub in his bathroom, and Doggy-dog, his favorite stuffed toy, lay on the pillow in his bedroom. Not that he noticed. He was asleep even before she had him into his pajamas. Even so, she lingered by his bed for a while.

This, she thought, watching the even rise and fall of his chest by the dim light of a bedside lamp, was what her marriage was really all about. Not the absurd jolt of awareness every time she looked at her husband, or the electric shock of his touch, but the simple pleasure of watching her son sleep and the knowledge that his future was secure at last.

Almost nodding off herself, she didn't realize she was no longer alone until a hand closed over her shoulder. "How's he doing?" Raffaello asked in a low voice.

"Fell asleep without a murmur."

"Same with Elisabetta. She didn't last past the first page of her bedtime story. How are you holding up?"

"Pretty well, all things considered." She ventured a glance at him. The lamplight played over his beautiful face, highlighting his classic cheekbones but leaving his eyes shadowed. "I learned more about you in ten minutes' conversation with your mother, than I did in the entire time I've spent alone with you."

"Anything you wanted to know, you only had to ask. I have no secrets."

She shrugged, the weight of his hand on her shoulder oddly comforting. "The opportunity never arose. We rushed from one thing to another with scarcely enough time in between to breathe, never mind get better acquainted."

"Now that you're more fully informed, have you decided you made a mistake in marrying me?"

"No," she said, too weary to feign indifference. "I just hope *you* don't live to regret marrying *me*."

"Why would I, Corinne? You're a level-headed woman, a devoted mother and exactly the sort of maternal influence Elisabetta needs in her life."

"What about what you need, Raffaello?"

The words swam out into the room so unexpectedly that she almost looked around to see who'd spoken them. But he never entertained a moment's doubt as to their origin. "What are you really saying, Corinne?" he inquired, tugging her to her feet so that she stood facing him. "That you'd like to renegotiate the fine print of our marriage agreement—which is to say, that part that has nothing to do with our children and applies only to you and me?"

"No, of course not," she muttered, stumbling over her answer and desperately hoping the lamplight was dim enough to hide the furious blush flooding her face. "I just want you to get fair value for your money…if you know what I mean."

"I'm not sure I do," he said, drawing her into the equally dimly lit dayroom connecting the two bedrooms. "Why don't you try spelling it out for me?"

Even though she felt hot all over, she was trembling like a leaf. "You're doing all the giving," she whispered. "I want to give a little, too."

"How? Like this?" He dipped his head and once again touched his mouth to hers. "Or had you something more intimate in mind…like this?" He slid his finger in a straight, sure line past the pearls at her throat, and cupping a brazen palm over her breast, teased her nipple with his thumb.

A sharp, sweet arrow of sensation speared the length of her and found its target between her legs, leaving her embarrassingly damp. Aghast, she stammered, "Only if it's what you want."

He put her from him as if he suddenly found her repugnant. "Sorry, Corinne, that's not a good enough reason. The day—or night—has yet to come that I take a woman to my bed because she feels she owes me her body."

She recoiled as if she thought he might hit something, and she wasn't too far off the mark. The urge to smash his fist against the wall rose in him strong and violent. Not that he'd make much impression on the wall, but the pain he inflicted on himself would at least put paid to the erection he couldn't control.

Touching her soft, warm curves, even so briefly, had left him half-blind with frustrated desire. But it was what *she'd* touched that inflamed him to anger. She'd touched his heart, making inroads where she had no business being, and *that* he found insupportable.

Brusquely he said, "It's past the dinner hour and we've kept my mother and aunt waiting long enough, so pull yourself together and get rid of the wounded deer look. Can you do that, do you think?"

She lifted her head and stared him straight in the eye. "I can do just about anything I put my mind to. I married you, didn't I?"

He'd have laughed if he hadn't been so incensed. "Yes, you did," he said. "Fine print notwithstanding."

Nose in the air, she swept past him and down the stairs with an hauteur that would have done a duchess proud, reaching the hall just as Malvolia and Leonora were making their way into the dining room.

"So sorry to have kept you waiting," he heard her say, joining them and leaving him to trail three paces behind like a mere consort.

He had to hand it to her. Whatever her private thoughts on him and what had transpired between them, not a hint of it showed on her face or in her manner during the meal. She sat opposite him at the long table, composedly sipped her wine, displayed a professional appreciation for the soup and excellent swordfish *involtini* which followed, admitted she had a sweet tooth and somehow managed to avoid addressing a single word directly to him, leaving Malvolia and Leonora none the wiser.

"I find her rather engaging," his gentle aunt declared, after Corinne had begged off joining them for coffee and gone to bed. "She has manners and a quiet self-assurance which is very becoming."

His mother nodded. "Nor is she afraid of hard work, and that speaks well of her."

"She's not overly impressed with my assets, either," Raffaello said, smiling grimly at the irony only he knew lay in his reply. Not only did Corinne appear indifferent to him as a man, but she'd shown remarkably little curiosity about his material wealth, which probably explained her almost fearful reaction when he'd shown her aboard the corporate jet that afternoon.

"This is *yours?*" she'd whispered.

"Yes," he said, and left it at that. She'd eyed the Gulfstream's plush interior so nervously that he hadn't had the heart to tell her he owned another jet, even larger.

"So your work involves a lot of travel?"

"Quite often, yes."

"If you don't mind my asking, exactly what is it that you do? Beyond the fact that you were married to my best friend and fathered a daughter with her, and have shown incredible generosity to me and my son, I know next to nothing about you."

"I have a few real estate investments," he said offhandedly, seeing no reason to mention that they were scattered over most of Europe. "I also have agricultural holdings in Sicily, and I like to keep my finger on the pulse of our chocolate factory."

"Chocolate factory?"

"That's right. It's been in my family since the early twentieth century. Sicilian chocolate is among the best to be found anywhere. We export ours all over the world."

"Chocolate's one of my secret indulgences," she confessed. "But then, you probably already figured that out, when I practically attacked that divine chocolate mousse you served me in your hotel suite in Vancouver."

He'd smiled. "I remember."

"Were you shocked?"

"Why would I be?"

"It's not fashionable for women to wallow in dessert. We're supposed to care more about being thin."

Considering she probably didn't weigh more than fifty-five kilos at the most, she could afford to wallow. "I've never been particularly taken with bone racks," he said. "Women were designed to have curves."

"How very nice of you to say so. You're a born diplomat."

She'd obviously changed her mind on that score. The cool glance she'd sent his way as she'd said good-night had made it clear she found him little more than a barbarian. It was enough to goad him into climbing into the big bed in the master suite, just to rattle her composure and show her who really had the upper hand.

But he wasn't willing to risk doing so. One rejection a night was enough.

Not about to give Raffaello the chance to snub her a second time, Corinne prepared for bed, then crossed the hall to the nursery wing. Despite her earlier nap, she was so tired she could have slept standing up if she had to, but a leather recliner in the corner of Matthew's room offered more comfort. With the blanket and pillow she found on the top shelf of his closet, she'd manage well enough spending the night in the chair.

She was just drifting off when *he* showed up, opening the door just wide enough for the light from next door to slice across her face and make her blink.

"What the devil do you think you're doing in here, Corinne?"

"I'd have thought it was obvious that I'm trying to sleep," she hissed, shading her eyes with one hand. "And avoiding you," she added for good measure. "Now go away and leave me alone. I'm in no mood to argue with you."

"Nor I with you," he said snottily. "It's not my style to waste breath trying to reason with an adult bent on behaving like a child."

And before she could drum up a quelling response, he tugged the blanket away and hauled her over his shoulder with about as much dignity as he'd afford a sack of potatoes.

Outraged, she squeaked, "Put me down this instant—"

He pinned his forearm across the back of her knees and maneuvered the pair of them out of the room. "Stop screeching, unless you want to wake the boy and have half the household coming to investigate," he advised.

If the prospect, particularly of the latter, wasn't enough to rob her of a coherent reply, the scent and feel and upside-down view of him certainly were. Not that he allowed her much time to enjoy the ride. Scarcely were they inside the master suite than he dumped her on the floor and impaled her in a glare that might have had her quaking in her shoes if she'd been wearing any.

"Let me make clear my expectations of you," he said, spitting the words out like bullets. "No matter how annoyed with me you might be, you will not make a public spectacle of our marriage in front of my family or my household staff."

"If that's what I'd had in mind, I'd have done something about it at dinner."

"That you chose not to was a very wise decision."

His ominous tone chilled her. "Is this what our so-called marriage is all about?" she asked, almost managing to keep her voice steady. "Your issuing orders and my meekly accepting them?"

"No," he said. "It's about a man and a woman working together for the good of their children. For that reason alone, I expect us to present a united front during the day."

"What about at night?"

"At the end, when Lindsay needed professional care, I turned my upstairs study into an extra bedroom for a nurse. I shall sleep there."

"Won't that give the household staff something to talk about?"

"No. It connects to this suite directly from the outside hall and opens into my bathroom. Only Patrizio, my valet, has access to it and his discretion is absolute." He brushed one hand against the other. "So you see, *cara mia,* your little drama was quite unnecessary. You may sleep in the master bed secure in the knowledge that your virtue is safe."

Swallowing what tasted horribly like disappointment, she said airily, "Well, that's a relief."

He headed for the dressing room door, then turned at the last minute and, with deadly accuracy, fired a final shot. "For both of us, I assure you. *Buona notte,* Corinne."

She really didn't expect they'd smooth over their disagreement as easily as he seemed to believe, but when she and Matthew came into the sun-filled breakfast room the next morning, Raffaello looked up from his newspaper and greeted her as if nothing untoward had occurred the night before.

"I'll introduce you to the staff and show you around the neighborhood later on, if you feel up to it," he offered her, as she fixed fresh fruit and cereal for Matthew at the buffet on the sideboard, and helped herself to coffee and yogurt. "The sooner you know your way around, the sooner you'll feel at home."

"What about your work? Surely you must be anxious to get back to it, after being away for so long?"

"It's Sunday, Corinne," he said, lifting Matthew onto a chair. "And I always reserve my weekends for my wife and children."

She glanced at her son busily devouring his cereal. "Well, speaking of feeling at home, I'd like to unpack the cartons you shipped over for us. Can we perhaps leave meeting the staff until this afternoon?"

"Of course." He eyed her appraisingly. "But give some thought to how you want things done around here. As mistress of my house, these are now your decisions to make."

"I'm in no hurry to make any changes, Raffaello. My being here at all is enough of an adjustment for your mother. Where are she and your aunt, by the way?"

"At the stables, with Elisabetta."

"Already? It's barely eight o'clock."

"They're early risers." He snapped his newspaper shut and refilled his coffee cup from the silver urn on the sideboard. "On weekdays, Elisabetta has classes from nine o'clock until two, so she has to be up early if she wants to spend time with her pony."

Matthew looked up from his cereal. "I want a pony, as well."

"Matthew, that's not polite," Corinne scolded.

Raffaello, though, shrugged off her reproach. "Every boy should have a pony, *figlio mio*. Your mother and I will see what we can arrange."

"You're going to end up spoiling him if you keep this up," she said quietly.

"He deserves a little spoiling. You both do. And if I can provide it, I see it as my duty to do so."

Later, as she was on her hands and knees arranging Matthew's favorite books on the shelf in his room, she glanced over her shoulder and found Elisabetta hovering in the open doorway. Again, the child's face told all, but if it wasn't exactly beaming with pleasure, Corinne, who'd been wondering how she could finagle some time alone with her without being too obvious about it, wasn't about to turn down a heaven-sent opportunity when it landed in her lap.

Smiling, she said, "Hi, sweetie."

"What are you doing?" Elisabetta asked mistrustfully.

"Just putting some of Matthew's books and toys away. Want to have a look?"

"No. I've got my own books and toys."

Oh dear, talk about getting off to a roaring start. "What if I told you I brought something for you, too. Would you like to see that?"

A flicker of curiosity flared in her stepdaughter's eyes. "I guess."

Standing up, Corinne brushed her palms together, and resisted the urge to take the child's hand. No point in pushing too hard, too soon. "Come on, then. It's in my room."

She led the way across the wide hall and into the sitting room of the master suite, where contents from half a dozen cardboard cartons were strewn about. "Here it is," she said, taking a flat box about the size of a paperback from the coffee table.

Elisabetta dropped down onto the sofa, opened the box and stared at the silver-framed photograph inside. "Who is it?"

"Your mother, Elisabetta, when she was just a few years older than you are now."

"Is it yours?"

"Yes. But I thought you might like to have it."

The girl traced her finger over the laughing face in the photograph. "She was pretty."

"Just like you, sweetie. You look a lot like her, you know."

"That's what Papa always says, but he doesn't have any pictures of her when she was little."

"I know. That's why I also brought lots of other photographs with me. They're in those albums over there. You can look at them any time you want, and if there are some you'd like to have for yourself, I'll get prints made for you."

"How come you have so many pictures of my mama?"

"She was my best friend, Elisabetta. We were like sisters. We did everything together, and I loved her very much."

"That's why Papa brought you here, isn't it?" Elisabetta cast her a sideways glance. "Because Mama wanted him to."

Corinne nodded. "Yes."

"But not because you wanted to."

"That's not true. I wanted very much to get to know my best friend's little girl."

"Maybe...but that doesn't mean you can be my mother."

"I know that, sweetheart. In fact, another reason I came here is to tell you everything I know about your real mama and make sure you never forget her. But even though I can never take her place, I want *you* to know that you can always come to me if something's troubling you, or if you want to talk about your mama. I have so many stories to tell you, when you're ready to hear them."

"And you'll let me look at your photographs whenever I want?"

"Absolutely. Just ask, and I'll get them out for you."

Elisabetta chewed her lip thoughtfully. "Matthew calls my father Papa. What am I supposed to call you?"

"Why don't we start with Corinne, and see where we go from there?"

"Okay." She picked up her framed photograph and with stilted formality said, "*Grazie* for the present. I'm going to show it to Papa now, then put it beside my bed."

Winning this little one over wasn't going to be easy, Corinne realized, watching as the child made her sedate way from the room. Unlike Matthew, who had no memories whatsoever of his father, Elisabetta remembered her mother all too well, and Lindsay was a hard act to follow, as Corinne very well knew. But at least she'd made a start, and that was something. As for what came next, she could only hope patience and affection would work in her favor.

Raffaello was as good as his word when it came to doing his duty by his new family. In fact, Corinne grew quite tired of hearing about duty in all its many applications. He made it his duty to familiarize Corinne with the outlying areas of his land which covered several hundred acres. Considered it his duty to show her the most pleasant places to walk, the path at the southeast corner of the property that led to the village, the steps descending to the beach.

Over her objections, he gave her a car, a dark blue Porsche Cayenne SUV, small enough to navigate the narrow streets of the nearby towns, and sturdy enough that she didn't have to worry about taking the children out in it.

"This is your home now," he told her, dropping the keys into her hand. "Yours to explore as you please. One thing I caution you against, however. Do not venture off-road behind the stables. This is not Vancouver, with its wide, well-lit streets and avenues. The land to the north of us is wild and treacherous."

"For heaven's sake, Raffaello!" she exclaimed in horror. "Matthew and Elisabetta roam all over the place unsupervised."

"But always on fenced Orsini land, and always within sight of someone who works for me. No harm can come to them here."

He introduced her to the stable hands, in particular Lorenzo, his head groom, a friendly, capable man who was married to Lucinda, the nanny. "What he doesn't know about horses isn't worth knowing in the first place," Raffaello said. "He'll choose the right pony for Matthew and teach him to ride."

One day, about three weeks after her arrival on the island, he took her to Modica, a beautiful old town originally dating back to medieval times, which was destroyed by an earthquake at the end of the seventeenth century and rebuilt over the next several years. After touring the chocolate factory, they climbed one of the many flights of steps connecting the lower and upper parts of the town, and stopped in a tiny family-style restaurant where he ordered mouth-melting *mpanatigghi,* a pastry turnover filled with minced meat mixed with cacao, "to satisfy your chocolate craving," he said.

"Considering how much I already sampled at the factory, I'll have put on ten pounds by the time we get home," she protested.

But he dismissed her concern. "You'll work it off this afternoon. You can't come to Modica and not see the churches of San Pietro and San Giorgio, or the Castle of the Counts."

The churches were magnificent; opulent and imposing, with their intricate carvings and gold-painted interiors. And although the climb to the ruined medieval castle just about killed her, it was worth the effort for the stunning view of the town itself, nestled on the slopes of the Iblei mountains.

"I want to come back another day and explore the shops," she sighed, when at last they headed home.

"Get my mother and aunt to bring you. They know the best boutiques, and you could use some new clothes."

"I can't afford them," she said, flushing. She knew well enough that, compared to Malvolia and Leonora, her wardrobe was inadequate, but the little money she'd made when she sold her business, she'd put aside for emergencies.

"*Dio*, Corinne, how often do you need to be reminded that you can now afford whatever your heart desires?" he said irritably.

"I don't feel comfortable taking your money."

"Why ever not? You're certainly earning it."

That much, at least, was true. Elisabetta had bonded quickly with Matthew, but was less easily inclined to allow Corinne to grow closer. As for Malvolia, she was a pain in the neck, forever undermining Corinne's authority with the children. Until the day she went too far.

"They are *bambini*," she insisted, upon hearing Corinne had banished both children to their rooms for trampling a flower bed to ruin. "God's little miracles and *perfecto*. You're too hard on them, Corinna."

"They're little miracles with more mischief between them than a wagonload of monkeys, Malvolia."

"They have spirit."

"They have ears, too, and it's not good for them to hear us disagreeing about how to handle them. We should present a united front."

"*Si, si!*" Malvolia sighed and flung out her hands. "You are right, *cara,* and I am an opinionated old woman who must learn to keep silent."

"That's not what I meant at all," Corinne said hastily. "Really, Malvolia, you have every right to your opinion and

I don't expect you always to agree with me, but please, let's not sort out our differences in front of the children."

"It won't happen again. You have difficulties enough as it is with my granddaughter who is not making things easy for you. I'm afraid my son expected a very great deal when he brought you here to stand in for Lindsay. I could hardly blame you if you've since come to regret marrying him."

"I have no regrets," Corinne replied fervently. "Raffaello is the finest man I have ever known, and nothing will ever make me go back on my promises to him."

"Santo cielo!" Malvolia regarded her with something approaching wonder. "I begin to think you care more for my son than you'd like him to know."

She was right. Without ever intending to do so, Corinne had started to fall in love with him. What had begun as sheer physical attraction had deepened to a more simmering passion, to a richer appreciation that went far beyond his startling good looks.

Raffaello Orsini was a man of many layers; of principle and intellect and an abiding respect for all living creatures. Considerate employer, charming host, devoted son and nephew, loving father, he assumed all roles with consummate ease, comfortable in his own skin, tolerant of those less capable, and indefatigable in the face of adversity.

Yet, it wasn't enough for her. For all they made a show of going upstairs and into the master suite together, she might as well have been living in a nunnery. And if truth be told, she was tired of it.

She was married in name only to this beautiful, sexy man who treated her with faultless courtesy, was wonderful with her son and who, with little more than the stroke of a pen, had elevated her overnight from exhausted, under-paid drudge to lady of leisure. And that's as far as it went. He didn't try to kiss her and he didn't touch her. Not by accident, not in the casual way that ordinary people touched one another—on the hand or the arm, in passing. He was simply there, and the distance he maintained between them tormented her as she lay alone in her big lonely bed every night.

He was her husband, yes. But not really. Not in the way she most wanted him to be.

CHAPTER SEVEN

"I HAVE TO GO away next week," Raffaello announced at dinner one night, toward the middle of March.

Corinne wasn't particularly surprised. He quite often went off on business, bearing out what he'd told her early on, that he traveled a fair bit.

"Where to, this time?" his mother inquired.

"Firenze." Then, with a glance at Corinne, "Florence, to you."

"Firenze, city of art and all things romantic." Leonora sighed dreamily. "Alphonso and I honeymooned there."

Across the table, Malvolia paused in the act of scooping a fat prawn from the excellent Sicilian fish stew Filomena had prepared, a little smile curling her mouth. "Now's your chance to do the same, Raffaello. Take Corinna with you and spend a few extra days showing her the city. You'd like that, wouldn't you, Corinna?"

Forestalling Corinne's reply, he said in a tone suggesting he'd rather undergo root canal therapy than be saddled with his wife's undiluted company, "Not possible. I'll be gone only two days, and in meetings most of that time."

"Even if you weren't, I wouldn't leave the children," Corinne said, cut to the quick by his rejection.

Malvolia pursed her lips and puffed out a dismissive little breath. Ever since their dust-up, she'd been much more cordial with Corinne, even though she did still spoil the children, every chance she got. *"Non dire sciocchezze!"* she said. "Such rubbish I never before heard. Leonora and I will look after the children, meetings don't last all night and Corinne's seen nothing of Italy. Firenze would be a wonderful place for her to start."

He heaved a defeated breath. "Would you like to go with me, Corinne?"

"No," she said, meeting his gaze and thinking he looked positively hunted. "I'd rather stay here with Matthew. It's not as if you and I would see much of each other."

"True, but you'd have no trouble keeping yourself entertained. Quite apart from the museums and churches, which would take years to explore in depth, you could go shopping for clothes." His glance skimmed over the black dress she regularly wore to dinner. "Perhaps you'll find something more to your taste in Firenze than you have in Modica."

Pride ought to have made her refuse. But where he was concerned, her pride more often than not took a beating. A smile, a conversation lasting more than a few minutes, a word of thanks for her continued efforts with Elisabetta, standing with his shoulder brushing hers as her son had his first riding lesson—such ordinary, everyday incidents were all it took to make her heart soar with hope that perhaps, in time, she and Raffaello would grow closer as husband and wife. Foolish hope because, despite his unfailing courtesy and remote kindness, he gave no indication he saw her as anything other than another addition to his stables. Her pedigree just wasn't quite up to the standard of his other horses.

"If you're sure I won't be in the way, then yes, I'd like to come with you. And," she added, flinging Malvolia and Leonora a quick glance, "if you're sure about looking after Matthew. I've never spent a night away from him before, so I don't know how he'll react."

"Matthew will be perfectly fine," her mother-in-law declared. "*You're* the one who'll fret about being away from *him,* but you may phone home whenever you please, just to reassure yourself that he's coping."

And so, on a warm, sunny morning, she found herself once again aboard the corporate jet as it headed northwest to Florence. Spring had come to the island. Although the mountains still had snow, wildflowers carpeted the valleys. The almond trees were in blossom, the vineyards being readied for the coming grape harvest.

From his seat beside her, Raffaello said, "Was leaving Matthew as difficult as you expected?"

"For me," she admitted ruefully, "but not for him. He's taken to the Sicilian way of life with a vengeance."

"And you, Corinne? How's it going for you and Elisabetta."

"Much better. She warmed up to me quite a bit after I showed her all the photographs of Lindsay and me, and really seems to enjoy hearing stories about when we were young. I think she's decided that if her mother liked me, I can't be all bad."

He shifted in his seat and, for a moment, she thought he was going to put his hand over hers. At the last minute, though, he merely rearranged his long limbs more comfortably, and tugged at the knife-crease in his gray linen trousers. "You've been very patient with her. Don't think I haven't noticed, or that I don't appreciate it."

"It's the least I can do, Raffaello, considering everything you've done for Matthew. He's never been happier."

"He's a good kid, and easy to love. Just ask my mother and aunt, if you don't believe me."

"Tell me about your meetings," she said, changing the subject in a hurry. As far as she was concerned, love—paternal, fraternal or in any other form—wasn't something she wanted to talk about with Raffaello. In her mind, her heart, the man and the emotion were too volatile a mix. "Are they about the chocolate factory?"

He shook his head. "No. They're to do with a breeding program I started several years back. I've always been interested in the Sanfratellani, a Sicilian horse whose history goes back centuries."

"Thoroughbreds?"

"Not in the usual sense, despite their distant Arabian and Thoroughbred bloodlines. They once roamed the northern slopes of the Nebrodi Mountains, but their numbers have greatly decreased so that, worldwide today, only a few hundred are alive, including eight in my stables."

"And you want to preserve the breed?"

He nodded. "I'm meeting with a consortium from Argentina who share my passion. Hopefully we can strike a deal that will benefit both horse and man."

"I don't know much about horses," she said. "I wouldn't recognize a Sanfratellani if I fell over one."

"You'd recognize mine. They're the black ones you admired, the first time I took you to the stables."

"Oh, *those!*" she exclaimed, thinking how long ago it seemed that she'd leaned against the fence beside him in the bright winter sunshine, impressed by the horses' graceful conformation and the satin shine of their coats. "I remember commenting on how handsome they were."

"Possessed of great stamina, too. With careful breeding, their numbers can be increased without sacrificing the qualities that make them so sought after."

"Are your colleagues already in Florence?"

"I hope so. Our first meeting is scheduled for this afternoon. I'll have time to check us into the hotel, then you'll be on your own until this evening." He reached into his briefcase and took out a handful of English language tourist pamphlets and a street map. "You might find these useful. They'll help you get oriented and give you some ideas of what there is to see and do."

"I appreciate your going to so much trouble," she said, touched by his thoughtfulness.

He shrugged. "I didn't," he said dampeningly. "They were my wife's."

And what does that make me? Corinne wondered miserably, as the jet began its descent over the Tuscan countryside. *An accessory after the fact?*

Oblivious to her distress, he pointed out the famous landmarks in the ancient city below. "…the Duomo… Giotto's bell tower….the Palazzo Vecchio…"

They could have been landing in Siberia, for all she cared. With just four words, he'd erased any magic the place might have held.

"Corinne?"

She looked up to find him watching her, the corners of his beautiful, sexy mouth twitching with amusement. "Hmm?"

"Did you hear a word I just said?"

"Yes." *As well as those you didn't say, such as I'll never amount to anything but a poor imitation of Lindsay.*

"So we'll meet back at the hotel around six?"

"Fine."

He unbuckled his seat belt as the jet cruised to a stop on the tarmac. "If anything changes before then, I'll leave a message."

Their suite, on the top floor of a hotel set in private gardens, which screened it from the city bustle outside its gates, offered a step back in history, and whatever else Corinne might think of Raffaello, she couldn't fault him on his choice of accommodation.

High eighteenth-century frescoed ceilings, period furniture and extravagantly swagged silk draperies all contributed to an air of refined elegance, but it was the attention to small details that made it all special. The bouquets of jasmine and roses that perfumed the parlor and bedroom; the toiletries and robes in the double en suite bathrooms; the bowl of fresh fruit on an inlaid rosewood side table; a sterling silver tray bearing champagne chilling in a sterling silver ice bucket. And from every window, breathtaking views of the city and the blue hills of Tuscany beyond.

And if all that wasn't luxury enough, their own private butler was on call, twenty-four hours a day. No question that as honeymoon locations went, the place took some beating. The only thing missing was the bridegroom.

"You can't have lunch before you leave?" she'd asked, trying very hard not to whine with disappointment when she saw Raffaello stuffing papers into his briefcase and heading for the door before the butler had finished unpacking their suitcases.

"Afraid not, but you'll be fine on your own. Pretty much everyone speaks English, Firenze's an easy city to discover on foot, and the hotel's close to the major art centers and shopping areas." He'd stopped just long enough to drop a brotherly kiss on her head. "Have fun, enjoy the afternoon and I'll catch up with you later."

The next moment, he was gone, only the faintest smell of expensive leather mingling with the scent of the flowers to signal that he'd ever been there. She was starving, but since eating alone under the vigilant eye of the butler held no appeal, she collected her purse and the tourist pamphlets and took the private elevator down to the lobby.

Leaving the hotel gardens by a side gate, she immediately found herself swept up in the ambience of the famous city. Its noisy, cheerful crowds, its colors and scents and stunning architecture, lent enchantment to her explorations as she wandered the narrow streets and sun-drenched piazzas.

She visited the souvenir shops along the Ponte Vecchio, and bought T-shirts and painted wooden pencil boxes for both children, as well as a model of the Duomo for Matthew, and a little gold bracelet hung with dainty filigree charms for Elisabetta.

Just before two in the afternoon, Corinne made her way to the Mercato Centrale, a huge indoor market housed under a nineteenth century glass and iron roof. In chef heaven, she browsed the array of multicolored pasta, cheeses, olive oils, balsamic vinegars and other gourmet foods displayed on the stalls. Finally she found an empty table at an outdoor coffee bar in a quiet square, and ordered a cappuccino.

She was pleased with her purchases, especially the charm bracelet, because she'd wanted to take something special home for Elisabetta. She hadn't exaggerated when she told Raffaello that her relationship with his daughter had improved. Lately, when Matthew climbed on her lap for storytime, Elisabetta inched closer, too, and leaned against Corinne, something she'd never done in the early days.

What he didn't know, because talking about it reduced Corinne to tears, was that she still had a long way to go in erasing the loneliness of a little girl who traced her finger over pictures of her dead mother, and whispered, "Mama was pretty, wasn't she?"

"Yes, she was," Corinne always replied, her heart aching for the child. "Just like you, sweetheart."

She'd finished her coffee and was debating making a quick visit to the Uffizi Gallery when Raffaello called her on her cell phone. "Glad you picked up," he began, sounding harried. "I've only got a couple of minutes, but wanted to let you know we're invited out tonight. Dinner with the Argentines at a restaurant in the country. Probably a high-end affair. Thought you might like advance warning."

Although the stone walls of the surrounding buildings glowed ochre in the afternoon light, at his words it seemed to her that a cloud had passed over the face of the sun. "Thanks for the heads-up," she said coldly. "I'll do my best not to embarrass you."

"*Dio,* Corinne!" His irritation fairly exploded in her ear.

"Give me a break, will you? I'm keeping you informed, that's all, not trying to insult you."

But trying to or not, he had. She didn't need to be reminded that the few dressy clothes she'd brought with her to Sicily were inadequate, and that it was past time she invested in a wardrobe more suited to the social circles in which she now moved. But when it came right down to spending his money on herself, she still hadn't been able to bring herself to do it. So she'd turned a deaf ear to his mother and aunt's offer to introduce her to their couturiers, and obstinately refused to use the credit cards he'd given her.

Until now, that was. *I'll fix him,* she thought, seething inside as she consulted her tourist pamphlets, paid for her coffee, gathered up her parcels and took a taxi to the city's fashion mecca, the chic Via Tornabuoni and Via della Vigna. She wouldn't give him cause to question her appearance again.

They were there in all their exclusive, ruinously expensive glory: Versace, Prada, Armani, Dolce & Gabbana, Bulgari. And somewhere amidst their dazzling one-of-a-kind display, she'd find something to make her reluctant husband sit up and take notice.

Three hours and thousands of euros she spent, selecting outfits for every conceivable occasion. With every stop, the number of purchases grew: smartly casual slacks and shirts, sportswear, afternoon dresses, glove-soft walking shoes and silk pumps with narrow, elegant heels. A floor-length silver-threaded dark red skirt and matching shawl for evenings at home. A gorgeously sophisticated sapphire-blue dinner gown to impress the Argentines. Purely for her own enjoyment, exquisite lingerie the color of whipped cream and peaches and midnight. And finally, for the sheer indulgence of it, a black velvet opera cape trimmed with Swarovski crystals.

She loved the feel of the lush fabrics against her skin, and how just the right cut and color turned her into someone she barely recognized. She'd knock Raffaello's socks off, or die trying.

She didn't try to delude herself, though. No amount of fancy window dressing could change the basic model. A natural blond, too tall and curvy to pass for petite, she might at best be considered nice looking, unlike Lindsay who'd been beautiful.

But for once, Raffaello would look at Corinne and see not the person he'd chosen to stand in for his dead wife, or the devoted mother working so hard to fill the empty place in his daughter's heart, but a woman in her own right.

"Hell hath no fury, and all that," she muttered, swanning out of the last atelier and stepping into the taxi the zealous doorman had hailed for her.

Once back in the suite, she stashed her purchases, then phoned the hotel beauty spa. The day had left her looking a little ragged around the edges, and the works was in order: body, face, fingers, toes and hair, she needed it all, and such was the clout of the Orsini name that she had no trouble securing an immediate appointment.

Raffaello paced the parlor, nursing a single malt scotch and trying to rein in his impatience. It was twenty after eight already, and the front desk had phoned to say the driver and car he'd ordered to deliver them to the country inn for nine, were waiting at the curb. Not that anyone would be too upset if they arrived a few minutes late, but he'd hoped he and Corinne would have time to smooth over their earlier spat before leaving. She, though, wasn't cooperating, and when she finally did put in an appearance, he was so stunned by her appearance that he could barely string two words together.

She'd done something different with her hair. Piled it on top of her head in a shining silver-blond coil. Painted her fingernails, which she no longer kept cut short, a rich, dark red. Applied something glossy to her mouth that made him want to kiss it. And she'd hit the boutiques with a vengeance. Long platinum earrings dangled from her ears. She wore heels. Very high heels, so that she stood only seven or eight centimeters shorter than him. Whatever dress she had on was hidden under a voluminous cloak of some sort that, if he hadn't known better, he might have thought was studded with diamonds.

"Er," he said, swallowing. "Um…I phoned the children. They're fine."

"I know," she said, sweeping past him, regal as a queen. "I spoke to them myself, not ten minutes ago. Come along, Raffaello. I'm sure you don't want to keep your important friends waiting."

So much for effecting a truce!

"You look nice," he said, eyeing her during the short ride down in the elevator.

"Do I?" she said snootily. "How kind of you to say so."

It took a lot to provoke him into cursing but, at that moment, he came close to uttering a few choice profanities. She quelled the urge with one forbidding blue-eyed glare.

During the drive to the restaurant, she sat as far away from him as possible—not exactly difficult, considering the limo's backseat was wide enough to accommodate four passengers with ease—her spine ramrod straight.

Willing to make one more effort to melt the ice, he said, "I gather you went shopping this afternoon."

"Very astute of you, Raffaello," she snipped back, and turned her head to watch the rural scenery flashing by, which she must have found riveting considering darkness had fallen hours earlier and the moon had not yet risen.

The last time a woman had left him at a loss for words, he'd been thirteen, and the daughter of one of the farm-hands had dragged him behind the stables, lifted her blouse to bare her breasts and offered to let him touch them. He'd been both fascinated and terrified by her audacity.

Corinne just plain irritated him with hers. Not inclined to sugarcoat his annoyance, he said baldly, "It's unlike you to be so out-of-sorts, *cara mia*. Did something you ate not agree with you?"

He'd have done better to keep his mouth shut. Very slowly, she turned her head to look at him, didn't seem to like what she saw, and very slowly turned her head away again. Shortly after, the car turned into the long driveway leading to the country house where they were to have dinner.

Wonderful, he thought. It promised to be a pip of an evening.

Nice. After all the trouble she'd gone to, to impress him, the best he could offer by way of a compliment was that she looked nice. *Nice!*

Well, she'd show him!

Their hosts, four men in all, stood at the window of a private dining room, but turned as one when she and Raffaello were shown in. If they weren't quite as handsome as Raffaello, they were nonetheless charmingly cosmopolitan. They kissed her hand and buzzed around her, plying her with champagne. They told Raffaello he was a lucky man, that his wife was *muy hermosa*—very beautiful.

In short, they did what he had not: they made her feel special, desirable. They flirted harmlessly with her, and she flirted back, lowering her lashes at their compliments and smiling over the rim of her champagne flute.

Across the beautifully dressed table, Raffaello leaned back in his chair and observed, something of a smile on his face, as well. Probably because she wasn't embarrassing him, after all, she thought, sparing him a brief glance before turning her attention back to the other four who seemed bent on learning everything there was to know about her life before she came to live in Sicily.

At first, he joined in the conversation, but as the evening wore on and one delectable course followed another, he grew increasingly grim, speaking only when addressed directly and keeping his replies brief and to the point. By the time the passion fruit gelato dessert arrived, his smile had grown fixed, and although his manner remained coolly and impeccably courteous, the light in his smoky-gray eyes hinted at a fire within.

Not until they returned to the hotel, though, did she learn just how savagely it burned.

CHAPTER EIGHT

THE ARGENTINES rode back to the city with them, dropping them off at the hotel, before going on to their own. Raffaello thanked them, bid them good-night and swiftly escorted her into the lobby. No trace of a smile, wooden or otherwise, remained on his face, nor did he speak during the short time it took the elevator to whisk them to the penthouse level.

"I had a good time tonight," she remarked, as the doors slid open at their floor. "I liked your friends."

He swung around, blocking her entrance to the sitting room and leaned into her, pressing her between him and the wall. His face was pale beneath his tan; the look in his eyes, frightening. "Did you really?" he said with such soft menace that chills raced up her spine. "What would it take to make you see me in the same benevolent light, I wonder? This, perhaps?"

He caught her chin firmly between his thumb and forefinger, abruptly tipped her head back and crushed her mouth with his. He tasted of rage and frustration and something else. Something dark and dangerous and intoxicating.

For a moment she resisted him, clamping her lips shut

against his invasion. A pointless exercise. She'd been yearning for him to pay attention to her for far too long to quibble about finesse when opportunity finally struck.

What counted was that he'd noticed her. Seen past the surrogate mother to discover the woman, and that was enough for her senses to swim. For her blood to churn. She went so weak at the knees that she had to clutch the satin lapels of his black dinner jacket to keep herself upright.

Then, as suddenly as it had started, it was over. He thrust her away and stepped back. Bosom heaving, she stared at him. Her lungs were seizing up, but he wasn't even breathing hard. "Or is that too crude for your sensibilities, Corinne?" he inquired icily. "Would I have more success if I kissed your hand instead? Would you then giggle, and lead me to believe you found me irresistible, the way you did with them?"

Incensed, she said, *"I did not giggle!"*

"You most certainly did." He inhaled a furious breath. "You giggled, and you simpered, and you hung onto their every word as if you couldn't get enough of their foolishness."

She shrugged flippantly. Better that, than let him know how badly she wanted to feel his mouth on hers again. "So what if other men find me attractive and I like it? Why do you care?"

"Because *I* do not like it," he said ominously. "I do not like it one little bit."

"Why not?"

"Because you're married to me, that's why."

She'd been baiting him all evening and knew her defiance now was pushing him to the limits of his patience. But she didn't give a damn. She was tired of living in limbo.

Either she was his wife in every sense of the word, or she wasn't. And tonight, she'd make him decide which it was to be.

"I'd never know it," she said.

"I could change your mind about that very easily."

Her pulse quickened. "I don't see how."

"By doing something I should have done weeks ago, *cara mia*. By reminding you whose ring you wear on your finger," he said, and cupping one hand at the back of her head, he kissed her again. A hot, openmouthed kiss that slid with devastating intent from her lips to the corner of her jaw, and from there to her throat.

Her hair came loose, tumbling around her shoulders, and then his fingers were at the closure on her cape. He yanked the garment free and let it slither in a whisper around her feet, then brought his gaze to dwell on the upper curve of her breasts, visible above the low-cut neckline of her gown.

"Now what?" she taunted. "Are you going to tear my dress away, too?"

"Would you like me to?"

"You wouldn't dare."

He made a sound low in his throat. A feral sound that should have terrified her, but thrilled her instead. "Try me," he ground out tightly.

He was beautiful in his raw anger, the most beautiful man she'd ever known, and she went at him like a starving woman, clawing at his fine dinner jacket, ripping at his bow tie, craving everything about him. Dying for him.

In a flash, he had her pinned against the marble wall of the tiny foyer once again. "This time, you push me too far, *streghetta,"* he hissed, and yanked the skirt of her gown up around her waist. The rasp of his zipper opening drowned out the faint screech of her panties as he ripped them away, and then he was between her thighs, probing at her flesh until, at last, he was where she'd wanted him to be almost from the first. Thrusting deep inside her, hot and silken and desperately trying to outrace the devils chasing him.

She whimpered and dragged his mouth back to hers again. Tasted the passion consuming him and responded to him with everything she had to give. Convulsing around him as he climaxed. Clinging to him as if she'd never let him go.

The aftermath made her heart bleed. Withdrawing, he rested his forehead against hers, and a tear leaked between the lashes of his closed eyes. *"Dio,* Corinne, I'm sorry...."

"No," she whispered, stroking his face. "Don't be sorry. I wanted this. You have to know I did."

He looked at her, and she saw the hell in his eyes, the self-loathing. "Never like that," he said. "Never in anger."

"How, then? Like this?" She took his hands and pressed them against her breasts so that he could feel how her nipples surged at his touch. "Or like this?" And she lifted her mouth to his and kissed him softly, deeply, the way a woman kisses the man she loves.

"You don't know what you're asking for," he groaned.

"Oh, but I do. I want to lie beside you at night. I want to hear you breathing and feel your warmth next to me. I want to be more than a mother to our children, Raffaello. More than your wife in name only."

He winced, his face the picture of a man in torment. "Corinne...!"

"Please." Her voice broke, her pride no match for the urgent, visceral ache of wanting him.

For a long minute, he stared at her, searching to find the truth of her words.

"*Please,* Raffaello!" she begged again. "Just for tonight, be my husband. You want to. I know you do."

She touched him. Cradled the weight of him. Felt his flesh stir again.

He cursed under his breath, then lifting her into his arms, he strode through the suite, and by the light of the moon riding high above the Tuscan hills, he took her to the bedroom, undressed her and did as she asked. Not hastily this time, but with dedication and a sort of despair, as if serving penance to some unholy god.

His mouth danced over her skin, discovering every inch with meticulous dedication. His touch left her floating in sensation. Ecstasy beyond description washed over her, wave after wave, each more tumultuous than the one before. She sobbed mindlessly, afraid she might die from the divine torture he inflicted. Wishing she would, because she was splintering apart, shards of her flying into orbit, and without him, she'd never be whole again.

Finally he possessed her a second time, so heavy and silken and potent that she shuddered. She raked her fingernails down his back, marking him hers, at least for that night. Locked her legs around his waist. Felt his muscles tense, and the tremors overtaking him. Heard his agonized breaths. Saw the sweat glistening on his shoulders. Felt him flooding into her, hot and powerful.

Then there was nothing but the calm hush of the night and the silent beat of their hearts.

Finally he rolled onto his side and lay on his back, his arm beneath her shoulder. She stole a glance at him and saw that his eyes shone like rain-washed stones in the moonlight, and his mouth was curved in unutterable misery.

If she had dared, she'd have told him he was wonderful, that he consumed her thoughts and filled her heart more than she'd ever dreamed possible. But then again, perhaps it was better that she did not, because where were the words to do justice to the enormity of all she felt?

There weren't any. They'd never before been spoken, or written, or thought. Nothing man had invented could come close to expressing the aching depth of her love for him.

He waited an eternity for her to fall asleep. At last, when her breathing had been deep and regular for nearly half an hour, he inched out of bed. Stealthily, like the thief in the night that he was, he left her. He had stolen her trust in him, betrayed his own code of decency and needed to cleanse himself of the guilt.

He dressed in the bathroom, then went from the suite, using the fire stairs rather than risk the discreet tone of the elevator wakening her. Once he gained the street, he turned at the corner, crossed the piazza and headed south to the river.

Firenze was as familiar to him as the back of his hand. He could have found his way in the dark anywhere in the city, but the sky to the east was touched with dawn when at last he reached the Ponte delle Grazie, to him the most beautiful of the bridges spanning the Arno.

At that hour, he had it to himself. A good thing. He wasn't fit company for man or beast.

How was he to face her again? How justify his behavior?

Mi scusi, Corinne, for yet another error of judgment. My fault. Too much champagne, I'm afraid, and not enough decent restraint....

The thing was, he'd taken no more than a glass or two of wine and couldn't blame his actions on inebriation. They'd arisen from something much more lethal. He'd been drunk on jealousy and rage, a combination more deadly than anything alcohol could induce.

This is my wife you're ogling, he'd wanted to bellow to the Argentines. *Get the hell away from her and find some other woman to drool and slobber over!*

That he hadn't, that he'd contained his fury with them, shamed him only a little less than that he'd vented it on her. He should have flattened the first man to step out of line and pinned him to the ground with a foot across the throat. Maybe that would have relieved the pressure building in him. Instead he'd waited until he was alone with her, then behaved abominably. Inexcusably. And, if he was honest, because he hadn't been able to help himself.

He'd believed Lindsay had been the love of his life and had neither wanted nor expected to feel that way again about another woman. Yet despite his most stringent efforts to deny it, with each passing day, each passing hour, his attraction to his new wife had grown.

At first, he'd put it down to proximity and tried avoiding her, hoping that, like a bothersome head cold, he'd eventually get over her. Instead he found himself more drawn to her, despite her letting him know in a dozen subtle ways that she wasn't interested in another husband. Why else had she spurned his generosity and persisted in wearing the plain, if not downright drab wardrobe she'd brought with her to Sicily? What other reason was there for her to hide her luscious body under clothes better suited to a nun, if not to remind him that she was Joe Mallory's widow far more than she'd ever be Raffaello Orsini's wife?

For weeks now, she'd used clothes to keep him at arm's length. Why last night had been different, he couldn't begin to fathom. Still, he'd curbed the hunger gnawing at him. Retained the upper hand over his libido—until the urge to brand her as his alone had driven him to near-madness.

He'd wanted to drown in her; to give her everything of himself. Instead he'd coerced her without mercy, overpowering her with brute force until she acquiesced instead of resisted, because compliance was preferable to stoking the rage he hadn't been able to control.

And now he had to live with the knowledge of what he'd done.

Close by, a church bell rang just as the sun rose high enough to bathe the skyline in golden light and glint on the restless water flowing beneath the bridge. No matter how much he wished it was otherwise, morning had come, and with it, the unenviable task of facing Corinne again.

She awoke to sunlight streaming through the window, and the delicious lassitude of a woman who, the night before, had been well and truly loved by the man of her dreams. Her body ached in places not mentioned in polite society, her skin burned slightly from the rasp of his jaw, her mouth felt swollen as a ripe strawberry. The scent of him lingered on the pillow next to her, on the bed linen and most of all, on her. She would never bathe again!

Nor would she ever forget how he'd looked, standing

proud and naked in the dim lamplit glow of midnight. Every sleek, sculpted curve and angle, from his broad shoulders to his long, powerful legs were forever etched in her memory, all elegantly gift-wrapped in dusky golden skin touched with dark, tempting shadows.

Reliving the sequence of events, her flesh pulsed again with echoes of rapture. The terrible risk she'd taken in stirring him to anger had paid off. The fire in his eyes had transmuted into a white-hot passion that refused to be satisfied. She couldn't wait for him to come back from wherever he'd gone so early in the day, so that they could do it all over again.

Stretching languidly, she drifted in a fantasy world. She'd open her arms and offer herself to him. They'd make love again, this time learning in the bright light of day the secrets the night had kept hidden. And in the sweet aftermath, she'd tell him the truth about everything: that her first marriage had been built on a foundation of infatuation and ultimately ended in disaster, but that she'd fallen irrevocably in love with him, Raffaello.

In turn, he'd admit that against all odds, he'd come to love her, too. That he couldn't imagine his life without her. That he was reborn, a whole man again, because of her.

The sound of the elevator doors whispering open sent her pulse roaring into overdrive. The moment was at hand.

He came directly to the bedroom and filled the doorway, a tall, well-dressed stranger regarding her as if he'd found an alien species in his bed, and she knew before he even opened his mouth that her happy ending wasn't going to happen.

"I'm glad you're awake," he said. "Corinne, we need to talk."

She cringed, all the stardust of the night before tainted by what she saw. No inner hell darkened his eyes. No tortured guilt, or bitter remorse touched his features, and certainly no eager pleasure. Rather, he remained so immune to emotion in any shape or form that she wondered how she'd ever managed to break through his defenses last night.

He dropped his leather jacket over the back of a chair, hooked his thumbs in the side pockets of his wheat-colored linen pants and came to stand at the foot of the bed. She knew what was coming next, could have recited the words for him before he even opened his mouth.

…terrible mistake last night…all my fault…can't be what you want me to be…wish I didn't have to hurt you…

She couldn't bear the indignity of it; the absolute humiliation of lying there naked beneath his cool, remote gaze. The only thing worse would have been his pity. She might have been swept off her feet by the events of last night, but his clearly had remained firmly planted on the ground.

Strike first and get it over with, the inner voice of self-preservation urged, and she seized on it as if it were all that stood between her and annihilation. Better a swift end, than a lingering death.

"If you're here to talk about last night," she said, dragging the shredded remnants of her pride around her, along with the bed sheet, "I'd just as soon not."

"At the very least, allow me to apologize."

"No need. I think it best we both forget whatever happened and move on."

"Can we do that, Corinne? Is it possible?"

Suddenly he looked haunted, and just as suddenly, she

was overcome with guilt. She'd pushed him into having sex with her. The least she could do was push him out and spare him flagellating himself for something that was entirely her fault.

"Certainly," she said, and steeled herself to degrade the most wonderful night of her life with a monstrous lie. "I wasn't myself and don't remember much of anything. Did we actually…?"

"Yes," he said grimly. "Twice."

"Really? I don't know what got into me."

A glimmer of bitter amusement flared briefly in his eyes. "I believe I did," he said. "I can only hope there'll be no lasting repercussions." He flicked a glance at his watch. "How soon can you be ready to leave?"

"For breakfast?"

"For the flight home."

"Don't you have more meetings scheduled for today?"

"My business here is concluded," he said grimly, "but if you wish to stay a few days longer, you're welcome to do so."

"That wouldn't say much for our so-called honeymoon, would it?" she said, amazed that she could sound so utterly in control when she was falling apart inside.

"Ours has never been your standard marriage. We each brought complications to the arrangement, some of which I don't anticipate we'll ever resolve."

"You mean, I don't fit your idea of the model wife. I'm not glamorous enough."

"You're a beautiful woman. But that you normally choose to hide behind nondescript clothing indicates to me, at least, that you don't wish to draw attention to the fact. You might as well have been wearing widow's weeds all this time—until last night when, for reasons known only to you, you decided to cast off your dowdy image. And look what happened as a result."

"It's a bit late in the day for regrets, Raffaello."

"Isn't it, though!" He stared bleakly around the room. "Well, do I instruct the butler to pack your bags, too, or are you staying on?"

"No. I've seen the sights and shopped till I dropped. Besides, I'm anxious to get back to Matthew."

"Then I'll meet you downstairs in an hour."

He flicked a disapproving glance to the floor, at the crumpled heap of sapphire-blue silk that was her gown, at her gorgeous French lingerie scattered like careless petals in a trail from the door to the bed and finally at one of her high-heeled shoes, sprawled indecently on its side, as wantonly depraved as its owner. Then without another word, he turned and left.

It was all she could do not to leap out of bed and fling herself at him. To hang on to his leg and beg him not to go. And knew that she could not, because nothing she did would change the facts.

The sad truth was, he didn't care about her, and he never would, at least not in the way she wanted him to. Not with gut-wrenching obsession and sleepless nights and endless mind games of "what if?" What if they'd met under different circumstances? What if he'd never known Lindsay?

She felt disloyal even entertaining such a thought.

When he'd first proposed marriage, she'd been afraid it might end up costing her more than it was worth. But she'd been thinking along the lines of self-respect and selling herself to a man willing to offer her more than she could

afford to turn down. Certainly she'd found him attractive,
irresistibly so. Any woman with half a brain would have.
But there was a world of difference between that, and falling so deeply in love with him that she'd crave whatever
attention he cared to toss her way.

She'd never dreamed she'd physically ache for him, morning, noon and night, so acutely that she'd cast aside every
shred of pride and resort to entrapment to gain her ends.
Never thought she'd beg him to take her to bed at any price.

In retrospect, of course, that was all he'd done. She had
wanted him to make love to her, but for him, it had been sex,
pure and simple. She'd been crazy to imagine, even for a
moment, it could ever be otherwise when he'd made it clear
from the outset that his heart belonged only to Lindsay.

The smartest thing she could do now was climb in the
shower, and scrub away every lingering trace of him from
her skin. The pity of it was, she couldn't erase him from
her mind and heart, as well.

CHAPTER NINE

THERE WERE REPERCUSSIONS. Even though she tried to ignore them in the weeks following the aborted honeymoon, Corinne had been through it all before and recognized the symptoms too well to be fooled into thinking she had the "flu"—or any of the other myriad ailments desperate women clung to when an unplanned baby was on the way.

Early pregnancy did not agree with her. She was tired, couldn't stand the smell of food and looked like hell. Morning sickness was an unkind myth perpetuated by men who thought having M.D. behind their names made them experts on all things female—or by women who'd never conceived a child. In reality, the nausea lasted all day long, sneaking up at a moment's notice and sending her scurrying for the nearest bathroom where she'd try to retch quietly, so as not to alert anyone else in the house to the true state of affairs.

Not that she needed to worry that Raffaello would notice anything out of the ordinary, because she wasn't the only one burgeoning with new life. Heavily involved in every aspect of organic agriculture, he was often gone from dawn to dusk, overseeing operations. The fields hummed with activity as vegetables of every size, shape and color ripened by the truckload. Although a year-round undertaking, most of the citrus harvesting took place between February and June. The Orsini vineyards, on the southernmost eastern tip of the island and lower slopes of Mount Etna, grew heavy with fruit, as did the olive groves, closer to home.

And if all that wasn't enough to keep him occupied, he spent days, and sometimes nights, at the stables, monitoring the health of his prize mare as she approached the end of a difficult pregnancy.

By comparison, Corinne didn't rate a second glance, and even if she had, he probably wouldn't have noticed anything amiss. In fact, no one did, because she did such a good job of hiding the evidence. Putting away all the pretty clothes she'd acquired in Florence, she reverted to the T-shirts and over blouses she'd brought with her from Canada. Supplemented by a couple of Muumuu-style sundresses that floated around her in loose folds, and a dinner dress with a dropped waist, she was able to disguise her condition well into her fourth month.

Part of the reason was that life in the house became more informal with the onset of hot weather. In June, the governess was sent home to her family in Calabria until September. At least once a week, Raffaello would steal a few hours away from other things to take the children to the stables and supervise their riding lessons. The rest of the time, Corinne organized picnics on the beach with them. She felt safe from prying eyes there, knowing that Raffaello was off taking care of business and that neither Malvolia nor Leonora would dream of tackling the steep steps leading down the cliff.

She'd strip down to the black bathing suit she wore under her concealing shirt and shorts, and wade into the limpid water next to Matthew as he dog-paddled in the shallows, or toss a ball to Elisabetta, who swam like a fish. They'd eat lunch in the shade of a big umbrella, and stay there until the worst of the day's heat had passed. Often, Matthew napped for an hour or two, worn out from all the activity of the morning, leaving Corinne free to work on cementing her bond with her stepdaughter.

Those were special times. Elisabetta would curl up next to her on the blanket and beg, "Tell me again about Mama when she was little."

"Which story today, sweetie?"

"The time that she cut her hair with the kitchen scissors," she'd say, or "When she fell in the goldfish pond," or "At the school Christmas play when she forgot her lines."

No matter how often Corinne repeated the stories, Elisabetta never tired of hearing them.

They also had many a solemn discussion about heaven and angels, and if Lindsay could see Elisabetta and knew that her hair had grown into pigtails, and that she could read.

"I'm sure she does," Corinne always replied because, accurate or not, it was the best comfort she could offer a child much too young to have lost one of the two most important people in her life. "Your mama is always watching over you."

Once the children were in bed, the adults usually ate dinner by candlelight on the bougainvillea-draped terrace. Raffaello was unfailingly polite on those occasions, dutifully asking Corinne about her day and commending her on her improved relationship with Elisabetta. In turn, she inquired after the new foal or, if he'd been away on business elsewhere, if he was pleased with the outcome. He'd made several trips overseas, once to finalize the purchase of a hotel in Paris, and another time to inspect a stallion on a horse ranch outside Buenos Aires.

"For stud purposes," he'd explained.

"You're thinking of shipping the poor creature all the way here just for that?" she'd asked, scandalized.

He'd burst out laughing, a rare occurrence ever since the trip to Florence. "No, Corinne, it'll be a long-distance love affair. In other words, by artificial insemination."

She both dreaded and loved those evenings. Dreaded them because she was terrified someone would make an issue of the fact that she hadn't touched her wine, or comment that she seemed to be putting on weight. And loved them because, for a few short hours, she could drink in the sight and sound of him, and pretend they were just like any other husband and wife. But the pleasure always ended up being tainted by the pain of knowing that when he looked at her, he saw only the woman who'd stepped into Lindsay's shoes.

The master suite was her sanctuary during those difficult weeks, the one place in the house where she didn't have to pretend about anything. She didn't have to hide her thickening middle. She didn't have to water the closest plant with her wine when no one was looking. She didn't have to put on a happy face and smile until her jaw ached.

She couldn't have what she really wanted, either, and sometimes wished she'd never agreed to her bogus marriage. But Matthew had taken to his new life like a bud opening in the warmth of the summer sun. He thrived on the organized routine, on the people who'd become constants in his life.

He and Elisabetta were inseparable, sharing everything: toys, people, animals, and until recently, even lessons in the little schoolroom at the back of the house.

Lucinda, Filomena and the rest of the household staff doted on him, sneaking him into the kitchen to eat cookies still warm from the oven. They taught him Italian, sang to him, called him their little prince. As for Malvolia and Leonora, he'd always had them wound around his little finger.

And Raffaello? However far he fell short of her hopes as a husband, Corinne couldn't fault him as a father. Although Joe had failed miserably in the role, she always tried to present him in a positive light to Matthew. After all, no child should have to grow up feeling ashamed of his roots. But when it came to a role model for her boy, she couldn't ask for a better man than Raffaello. From the first, he'd treated her son as his own, and Matthew idolized him, following him around the stables like an adoring puppy, every chance that came his way.

How could all that not be enough for her? How could she ask for more?

She knew how. Raffaello had reminded her that she was a woman still in her prime. He'd awoken her from the long, cold sleep of widowhood, and the memories of that one magnificent night in Florence haunted her.

Sometimes, she awoke in the night, crying. Sometimes she closed her eyes, hugged her pillow and pretended she was hugging him. And sometimes, she simply remembered. Remembered how he felt inside her; how he'd held her face between his hands and buried his mouth against hers. Remembered the sweat gleaming on his olive skin, and the passion in his beautiful gray eyes, and the frantic bursts of his heart beating against hers.

Sometimes, she thought he remembered, too. She'd catch him watching her, his expression veiled, and the atmosphere would sizzle with sudden awareness. Goose bumps would chase over her skin, her stomach would turn over, and a distant throb of awareness would settle between her thighs. But then, at other times, his gaze was oddly indignant, as if she'd offended him simply by breathing, and the thought of telling him she was pregnant horrified her.

She knew she was running out of time; that sooner rather than later, he'd have to know. But when he eventually did find out, it was in a way she'd never anticipated, and the fallout was about as bad as that following the night she'd conceived.

Sagra di metà, or high summer festival, was a local tradition somewhat similar to Thanksgiving. Since there was never a time that something or other wasn't being harvested on Orsini land, though, the celebration took place on a Saturday at the end of July, instead of in October.

The first Corinne heard about it was when Raffaello announced earlier in the week that she'd be attending it with him. The event, a night of music, dancing and feasting, was held in the village square, and considering that just about everyone living in the area worked for the Orsinis in one capacity or another, she figured there'd be quite a crowd.

"We'll be expected to put in an appearance, stay long enough to be seen enjoying ourselves and leave early enough that everyone can cut loose without the boss watching," he told her.

She understood exactly what he meant. The real Sicily was all about its people. About men and women who lived and breathed its fertile valleys and wild mountain terrain. About customs and superstitions going back hundreds of years. But even in the twenty-first century, a pronounced class distinction still existed. Raffaello might be highly respected by those he employed, but he played a very limited role in their personal lives.

Saturday night was hot, the air still and the sky a bolt of black velvet studded with stars, except where the reflection of lights from the festivities hung in the air like pearl-tinted clouds. She and Raffaello arrived at the party shortly after nine, walking along the gravel lane that began just past the boundary of his land and ended at a stile, about half a mile from the village.

When they finally reached the square, the scene reminded her of something taken from a movie. At one end stood the church, its stone facade washed with gold from the many lanterns hanging in the gnarled old olive trees. Huge vats of seafood stew flavored with garlic and capers simmered over a fire pit. Long tables covered in oilcloth groaned under the weight of other foods. Bread, something normally served only with the midday meal, spilled warm and fragrant from wicker baskets. Bowls of pasta vied for space with trays of roasted peppers, tomatoes, zucchini and eggplant.

Men playing accordions and tambourines filled the night with sound. At smaller tables placed randomly under the trees, people poured wine from painted stone pitchers and thumped their fists in time to the music, while in the middle of the square, couples of all ages danced a wild tarantella, the women wearing long, full skirts in vibrant shades of red and purple and green. Children and dogs darted among the shadows under the benevolent watch of grandmothers and great-grandmothers soberly clad in black.

For almost an hour, Raffaello mingled with the villagers, introducing Corinne as he worked his way from one group to the next. They sampled a little food, he drank a little wine and she did as usual, discreetly disposing of hers on the dusty ground.

Then, as the musicians struck up again, he took her by the hand and drew her into the crowd milling around the impromptu dance floor.

He hadn't touched her with any sort of familiarity since that night in Florence. To have him slide his arm around her now, over four months later, and smile down at her as if he was proud to call her his wife, filled her with such profound happiness that, even knowing it was an act put on for the benefit of those watching, she welcomed it. Was so desperate for him that she forgot to be careful, and went willingly into his embrace.

He spun her around, led her sure-footedly through some complicated country dance, laughingly pulled her close when she almost tripped over an uneven flagstone. And suddenly, with everyone else twirling madly around them in the flickering lantern-light, he stopped dead.

His smile faded. Very cautiously, he lowered his hands to the front of what had once been her waist and rested them there. As if he knew his father's touch, her baby moved for the first time with just the faintest flutter of acknowledgment. Raffaello couldn't possibly have felt it, but Corinne knew from the look on his face that she didn't have to worry about when or how to tell him she was expecting a baby. Her body had spoken for her. Very plainly.

"Raffaello—" she began.

"Do not say another word," he warned her, his lips barely moving. "Not now, and not here."

Then taking her wrist in an unforgiving grip, he wove a path through the other dancers, and with a deceptively nonchalant wave here and cheerful nod there, bid everyone good-night and practically frog-marched her back the way they'd come, less than two hours before.

The music and laughter had died to an echo when he stopped at the stile and swung around to confront her. By then, the moon had risen. Its cold light showed his mouth set in a thin, harsh line and turned his eyes black with disgust.

"Is there a reason you haven't shared your news with me before now?" he inquired, his voice a whiplash of contempt.

"I wanted to. I just didn't know how."

"'I'm pregnant' would have sufficed. Or, 'I'm expecting a child.' My English is more than adequate to grasp the import of either statement."

"They aren't words you wanted to hear."

"What I want, Corinne, is the truth. Preferably before I find myself the laughingstock of the whole of Sicily."

"What truth?" she said, bewildered.

"Is it mine?" He fired the question at her, lethal as a bullet aimed straight at her heart.

Reeling from the impact, she grabbed blindly at the stile and stared at him, shell-shocked. "Yes, it's yours," she said with quiet dignity when she could trust herself to speak. "And I will never forgive you for suggesting otherwise."

He had the grace to look ashamed. "What is it about

you, that makes me want to hurt you?" he muttered, dragging his hand down his face.

"You resent me because I'm not Lindsay."

"I don't expect you to be."

"Yes, you do, and I've had enough of it. I loved Lindsay dearly and still miss her to this day, but I'm really not interested in spending the rest of my life trying to measure up to her."

"Then we are of the same mind, since your closing your beautiful blue eyes and pretending I'm your dead husband when I kiss you, doesn't work for me, either."

"Fine, then! Let's put this farce of a marriage out of its misery, and end it once and for all."

"That is not an option, nor will it ever be, as you have known from the outset. We married for the sake of Matthew and Elisabetta. Now we have a third child on the way. Does this baby not need us just as badly as the other two?"

"What about what you and I need?" she cried. "How long can we go on pretending to the whole world that our marriage is real, when we both know you care more about your blasted horses than you ever will about me? I'm tired of always running second best, Raffaello—almost as tired as I am of living a lie."

"Then we have to try harder. Start over. Make a better beginning."

"How can we, when I know you don't want another child?"

"How do you know that?"

"Because you said, in Florence, after…that night, that you hoped there wouldn't be any repercussions, and… well…there are."

"Indeed." He nodded. "Which leads me to ask, do you regret that you're pregnant?"

"No," she said, and wished she dared tell him that having his baby was the next best thing to having him tell her he loved her.

"Then since we are baring our souls at last, let me tell you that I am tired, too. Tired of fighting the inevitable where you and I are concerned. I am not made of stone, Corinne. You are a beautiful woman, and I'm—"

"A hot-blooded Sicilian who won't spurn my advances," she finished bitterly. "Yes, you made that clear, the first time we met. Unfortunately you were anything but pleased when I took you at your word. Or have you forgotten our blighted attempt at a honeymoon?"

"You caught me by surprise. But I am willing to give us another chance, and so should you be. There are, after all, much less pleasurable obstacles to overcome than physical intimacy, when trying to make a marriage work."

"Are there?"

"I am sure of it."

"Right now, I'm not very sure about anything."

He unclipped his phone from his belt. "Because you are overwrought," he said, in the kind of soothing tone he might use on a highly-strung mare. "The evening has been too much for a woman in your condition. I shall call for a car to take us home."

"No need. I can walk back."

"No, *cara mia,* you cannot. The path is too rough. You must take better care of yourself now. On Monday, I will arrange an appointment for you with a doctor in Modica."

"I already have a doctor in Modica. An obstetrician, in

fact, who assures me I'm as healthy as a horse." *Just not as important as one.*

"I would like to hear that for myself."

"If you must," she said, all at once weary of the whole unhappy mess they called a marriage. Why was it, she wondered, that after weeks of pining for his undivided attention, she found herself so dissatisfied, now that she'd got it?

She knew why. He'd very kindly given her a handful of stars, when what she wanted was the moon. Well, too bad. The moon wasn't to be had, and that was that.

"I must," he said. "As your husband, it is both my right and my duty."

Ah yes, she thought bleakly. *That word "duty" again.*

He punched in a number, relayed his request for a car and during the few minutes it took for it to arrive, tucked his arm around her shoulder and pulled her close.

She sank against him, too exhausted to fight him, or herself, any longer.

Malvolia cornered her the next morning at breakfast. "Raffaello has told me," she said. "It is wonderful news."

"You think?"

A small silence followed then, to her surprise, Malvolia reached across the table and took her hands. "You and I have had our differences, Corinna, and I confess that, in the beginning, I was not in favor of my son's marrying you so hastily. I did not think it fair to you, to him, or to Elisabetta."

"You thought I married him for his money."

"At first, I did, yes. He has so much and you clearly had very little, and I feared you would take advantage of his generosity. But that was in the beginning, and much has changed since then."

She squeezed Corinne's hands gently. "Corinna, I love my son and granddaughter deeply. They both have suffered greatly in the past and their happiness matters more to me than anything else. But you, my dear, have brought a harmony to this house which has been missing for a very long time. You are a wonderful mother who has taken Elisabetta into your heart with all the love and patience anyone could ask of you, and that, I know, has been no easy task. As a mother myself, I applaud you for that. But that you have proved yourself also to be a good and loving wife to my son is more than I ever dared hope to see. So if I haven't told you before how much I admire and care for you, then let my pleasure at your making me a grandmother again speak for me."

This, coming on top of last night's confrontation with Raffaello, was more than Corinne could bear. "Please don't be so nice," she wept, sobbing into her napkin. "I'm enough of an emotional mess, as it is."

"You're supposed to be, *figlia mia*. It's part of the process of cooking a new life."

At that, she choked back a laugh. "Then I should have a perfect baby."

"I'm sure you will." Malvolia tipped her head to one side, her dark eyes filled with concern. "And yet, I detect a sorrow in your heart. Why is that, Corinna? A baby you and my son have created together is a good thing for everybody, surely?"

"But not something we planned."

"What does that matter? Such things happen and you *are* married, after all."

"Raffaello's a very busy man. I'm not sure he really wanted another child."

"Nonsense! He's never too busy for his family, and I can tell you without fear of contradiction that he is overjoyed at becoming a father again."

Which is more than she could say for her late husband, Corinne thought, shuddering at the memory of the day she'd told Joe that Matthew was on the way.

He'd looked as thunderstruck as if she'd admitted to burying a body in the back garden. "What do you mean, *we're* having a baby?" he'd snapped, glowering at her across the dinner table. "How the hell did you let that happen?"

"Well, it takes two," she'd reminded him.

"No, Corinne. It only took you, because you're the one supposed to be on the pill."

"And I was…except for the time I had the stomach flu."

"Well, your mistake, sweet cheeks, not mine."

Stung by his attitude, she said, "What are you implying? That I'm on my own in this and you want no part of our child?"

He'd relented a little at that, and she'd hoped that once he got used to the idea, he'd share her anticipation. And for a while, he had, taking pride in the evidence of his virility. "All I had to do was hang my pants on the back of the bedroom door, and bingo!" he'd boasted to his pilot friends.

Sure she'd give birth to a son, he already had a name picked out. "Matthew, after my dad, and Joseph, after me," he'd declared.

But when he discovered that regardless of its sex, a baby demanded attention almost twenty-four hours a day, fatherhood soon lost its luster. He started staying out late.

Sometimes didn't come home at all. "Mine's a high-stress job," he'd contended. "I need to relax in my off-time, and there's none of that to be found around here with the brat squalling half the night."

And then, suddenly, it was all over. Matthew started sleeping through the night, but it no longer mattered. Joe was dead, killed trying to land a float plane in heavy fog, at a remote fishing camp in northern B.C.

Within the year, Lindsay was dead, too. Which brought Corinne full circle to where she was today: married a second time and pregnant again—this time to a husband man enough to face up to his responsibilities without the need to lay blame on someone else.

If for no other reason than that, she had to agree with Raffaello. They must try harder to make their marriage work. Three innocent lives depended on it.

CHAPTER TEN

IN THE WEEKS FOLLOWING, she could hardly fault him for his efforts. He attended every doctor's appointment with her. Made sure she followed to the letter every instruction regarding vitamins, exercise, rest. Catered to whatever craving happened to be her flavor of the day. Chocolate-covered marzipan and tomatoes, one week; sardines and figs drizzled in balsamic vinegar, the next.

He massaged the small of her back when it ached. Worried if her ankles swelled. Commented if he thought she looked tired, so much so that she took to wearing sunglasses whenever possible, just to shut him up.

He insisted on buying her a maternity wardrobe extensive enough to keep six pregnant women in haute couture sophistication. Fine silk and cashmere skirts and slacks and tunic tops for daytime wear. Lovely flowing dresses in rich, gorgeous velvets for evening, some falling from the shoulder in straight simple lines and others with high empire waists and flattering necklines that dipped to reveal a hint of cleavage. Voluminous nightdresses and peignoirs of soft combed cotton trimmed in satin and French lace, that fell to her ankles and caressed her skin. Beautiful handcrafted suede shoes with heels high enough to be elegant but low enough to be safe.

He slept with her in the big master bed. Put his arms around her and kissed her good-night. Sweetly, softly, on the mouth. Even made love to her occasionally, with great tenderness and attention to her pleasure, rather than his own. But never with the untamed passion, the rampant desire he'd shown in Florence.

In other words, he went through the motions, but his heart wasn't really in it. She knew that because, if she moved too close to him in the middle of the night, he'd turn his back to her and inch to the far side of the mattress. If she reached over in the dark to take his hand and place it on her swollen belly so that he could feel the baby kick, he'd snatch it away again as if she'd burned him.

She could hardly blame him. What man wouldn't be repelled by a wife so bloated, she couldn't see her own toes anymore, and who waddled around like an over-stuffed penguin?

When he wasn't there to monitor her every waking breath, his mother and aunt stepped in, smothering her in affectionate concern.

"Don't go down to the beach anymore, *figlia mia*. You could fall on the steps and hurt the baby."

"Be careful with that heavy picnic basket. We don't want the baby arriving before his time."

"Put your feet up and look after the little one you're carrying, Corinna, and leave the other two children to us."

The baby this, the baby that… And because she was the sacred vessel entrusted to carrying it safely to term, she was treated like spun glass. It irritated her beyond words.

"I won't break," she snapped, when Raffaello suggested she shouldn't be tramping around the garden by herself when she was seven months along. "For heaven's sake, stop fussing and leave me alone!"

She didn't really want him to leave her alone. She wanted him to care about her, not just because she was pregnant, but because she was his wife. Besides, what did he think? That she'd deliberately do anything to endanger their child whom she'd loved desperately from the second she knew she'd conceived?

Then there were Elisabetta and Matthew, and their pointed questions.

"Why are you so fat?"

"Because there's a baby growing inside me."

"Who put it there?"

Not prepared to launch into a graphic explanation of how babies were made, she said, "It grew from a seed."

"How does it get out? Like a balloon bursting if you prick it with a pin?"

Dear God, she hoped not!

She enjoyed a slight reprieve in late autumn, with attention turned to the fall harvest. Nets were spread under the olive trees and as one army of workers hand-picked the crop, another filled baskets with the fruit and took them to the oil press. Orsini olive oil was exported worldwide, and very big business. No sooner was that task completed than it was time to pick the moscato grapes from which the yellow fortified Orsini wine was made. It, too, enjoyed an international reputation.

Glad something else was the chief focus of her husband's attention, even if only temporarily, Corinne devoted those weeks to assembling the baby's layette, making a point of including the children in the preparations whenever possible. Elisabetta and Matthew both had made so many amazing adjustments in their lives, and the last thing she wanted was for either of them, especially Elisabetta, to feel displaced by the new arrival.

She took them shopping when morning classes were over, and let them choose items for the baby's room. A lamp in the shape of a crescent moon, with star-shaped cut-outs where the light showed through. A framed print, a quilt, a musical mobile, a soft, cuddly teddy bear. And always, at the end of the trip, they'd get to choose a little something for themselves. A book, perhaps, or new crayons and thick pads of sturdy construction paper in a rainbow of colors.

Usually they went to nearby Noto, a beautiful little city of churches on the left bank of the River Asinaro, renowned for its eighteenth century baroque architecture. As long as she was home and dressed for dinner in one of her lovely gowns before anyone had time to miss her, no questions were asked about where she and the children had been, or how they'd spent their time.

Once, though, on a cool, overcast afternoon toward the middle of November, she drove as far as Modica. After browsing the boutiques along the main Corso, she treated the children to gelato in a little shop near the Church of Saint Mary of Bethlehem.

Elisabetta had been unusually quiet that day, leaving Corinne to wonder if she was coming down with something.

"When the baby comes," the child eventually asked, studiously poking her spoon into her ice cream, "what will it call you, Corinne?"

"Nothing," Corinne said. "Babies don't start talking until they're about a year old, as a rule."

"But when it does start, will it call you Mommy, the way Matthew does?"

"I expect so, yes."

"And Papa will be Papa?"

"Yes."

"So I'll still be the one left out," she said, and plopping down her spoon, burst into tears.

"Oh, sweetheart!" Finally understanding what lay behind the questions, Corinne pulled the little girl onto her lap—or what was left of it, these days. Although Matthew had claimed Raffaello as his own within days of arriving in Sicily, Elisabetta had never been able to bring herself to call Corinne "Mommy" or "Mama."

"I don't want the baby to live with us," she sobbed now. "I want Papa to send it to Canada."

"If he did that, my angel, I'd have to go, as well, and I'd miss you terribly. Not only that, this baby is really looking forward to having you for a big sister, and how could you be that, if we lived so far away?"

"I'm not going with you," Matthew piped up, between shoveling in mouthfuls of gelato. "I like it here with Papa and Nonna and Zia and my pony."

Disloyal little toad!

Not about to be distracted, Elisabetta whimpered, "I won't really be its sister, because you're not really my mother."

"But I love you as much as if I were," Corinne said, stroking her hair. "In my heart, you really are my little girl, just as much as Matthew is my little boy, and I promise you, you're definitely this baby's big sister."

The tears subsided gradually until just one stray was left to roll down the petal-soft cheek. "Really and truly?"

"Cross my heart."

"But how will it know?"

"Well, for a start, because you'll always be there, playing with it, and helping me to look after it. Only very important people like sisters and brothers get to do that. Of course, if you called me Mommy or Mama, then for sure the baby would know we all belong to the same family— but only if you want to."

"If I did, do you think Mama will mind?"

Had it been anyone but Lindsay they were talking about, Corinne might have sunk low enough to be jealous. But she understood all too well how unforgettable Lindsay was, even to the child she'd mothered for only three short years.

Stroking Elisabetta's hair away from her flushed face, she said, "I guarantee that if you're happy, your mama will be happy, too."

Elisabetta considered the matter gravely, then nodded, sending her pigtails flying. "Well then, p'raps I'll call you Mommy, like Matthew does, then it won't hurt Mama's feelings and she won't think I've forgotten about her."

"You're a very smart little cookie, Elisabetta Orsini. You just made your mama and me very happy and proud."

"I know." Confidence restored, she slithered off Corinne's lap and climbed back on her own chair. "I'll finish my gelato now so we can shop for our treats before we go home."

They stayed in town a good bit longer than Corinne intended, and arrived home after dark to find Malvolia and Leonora twittering like distraught sparrows, and a grim-faced Raffaello about ready to call out the equivalent of the national guard.

"Tell me, if you will, Corinne, what purpose there is in carrying a cell phone, if you do not have it turned on?" he exploded, the minute she set foot in the house. "I've been trying to contact you for the last hour or more."

"Why? Did something happen?"

"*Si,* something happened! You and the children went missing."

"Oh, don't be so melodramatic," she scoffed. "We went shopping in Modica, that's all."

"You think it melodramatic that my mother and aunt have been sick with worry? You think it unreasonable for a husband to show concern for a wife who disappears with his children, and says not a word to anyone about where she can be found or when she might return?"

"I'm sorry you're so upset. Time kind of got away from me, but as you can see, we're all perfectly fine, and no harm's been done."

"In your opinion, perhaps, but not in mine. You're thirty-six weeks pregnant, woman—much too far along to be driving such a distance. Look at you, so pale and exhausted. And in case you haven't noticed, it's raining. Hardly ideal driving conditions, especially after dark. What if you'd had an accident?"

"But I didn't," she said calmly. "I'm perfectly capable of looking after myself *and* the children, so please stop treating me as if I'm a half-wit who's never driven in rain before."

Unconvinced, he eyed her severely. "I want your word that you will not put yourself or the baby at risk like this again. If you must go to Modica, I or someone else in the household will take you. Promise me, Corinne."

"Oh, all right," she sighed, secretly quite happy to go along with his request. Contrary to her assertions, driving home along dark, twisting country roads, with the rain slashing across the windshield, had been downright nerve-racking at times, and she was more than ready to play the submissive wife in need of a keeper. "Is that all, *signor,* or may we go upstairs and change for dinner now?"

"I should punish the three of you by making you dine on bread and water in the kitchen," he growled, unable to keep his face as straight as he might have liked. "You've given me gray hairs before my time."

"You shouldn't talk to Mommy like that," Elisabetta scolded, skipping blithely past him. "Not when she's preggernant."

Astonished, he flicked a glance at Corinne and inquired sotto voce, "So it's 'Mommy' now, is it? When did this happen?"

"While we were misbehaving in Modica. You want to spank me for that, as well?"

Again, his mouth twitched in the beginnings of a smile. "An excellent idea, *mia moglie,* and one I'm sorely tempted to act upon."

"In your dreams!"

"You have what they call in America 'a smart mouth,' my dear."

"Just one of my many talents," she said breezily, and gathering up her purchases, trundled her bulk up the stairs after the children.

Later that evening, after Elisabetta and Matthew were in bed, and the adults gathered in the *soggiorno* for after-dinner espresso and brandy—all except Corinne who sipped a caffeine-free latte—he announced, "Tomorrow, I must go to Milano and shall be away for three days."

Disturbed, Malvolia set down her demitasse. "Is that wise, Raffaello, with Corinna so close to confinement?"

"What if the baby comes while you're gone?" Leonora added, making it sound as if a woman giving birth without her husband there to wipe the sweat from her brow was tantamount to treason. "Imagine if you were not here to see your son or daughter born."

"I hardly think that's going to happen. My due date's not for another four weeks," Corinne reminded the room at large.

She might as well have saved her breath. "It's a chance I'm going to have to take," Raffaello said. "I have matters urgently requiring my attention. If I could put them off, I would, but—"

Flaring up, she said, "There's no reason to put anything off. I saw Dr. Sabbatini just yesterday, and he's perfectly satisfied that everything is as it should be, and I'm right on schedule for the delivery."

"Nevertheless, any sign that that might change, and you are to contact me immediately. I can be home in less than two hours." Raffaello touched her hand briefly, making her ashamed of her irritation. "Nothing will keep me from your side when you give birth, Corinne."

He sounded so sincere, so much the devoted husband, she had to remind herself it was the baby he really cared about. Well, better that, than to be like Joe: utterly indifferent to everything but his own selfish needs and desires.

"I promise you, Raffaello," she said, curling her fingers around his, "nothing's going to happen."

"I'm counting on you to keep to that, *cara mia.*"

Once upon a time, when her understanding of Italian had been limited to the most basic terms, she'd have bloomed under the endearment. Now, she knew it carried none of the intimate clout associated with *amore,* or *tesoro,* and amounted to little more than an avuncular "my dear." Nevertheless, the way his gaze rested on her, so warm and concerned, caused her stomach to flip in a funny little somersault. Was it possible he *did* care for her, just a little bit?

"We'll keep a close eye on her," his mother promised.

"And make sure she doesn't overdo," Leonora chimed in.

Holding his gaze, Corinne went one step further. "If it'll ease your mind any, and if your mother and aunt don't mind looking after the children, I'll even promise to put my feet up and not lift a finger while you're gone."

Nods of approval all around made it clear she'd said the right thing.

"*Si,* it will ease my mind," Raffaello admitted.

That night in bed, he pulled her close and spooned his long body around her. "Remember, you are to be a very good wife while I'm away," he reminded her, his breath ruffling her hair and stealing warm and sweet over her nape.

Drowsy and safe in his arms, she said, "I will," and fell asleep, lulled by the steady thump of his heart.

Uncommonly heavy rain fell over the next two days and what had started out as a novelty for the children soon became a burden. Matthew, especially, chafed at not being free to race around outside and complained bitterly about missing his beloved pony. So when the sky cleared in midafternoon on the third day, and Malvolia and Leonora offered to take them to the stables, Corinne was happy to agree.

She couldn't wait for Raffaello to come home that evening. Although neither had said or done anything specific, she'd felt closer to him, that last night before he left for Milan, than she'd felt at any other time in their marriage. In the days since, she'd known a hopefulness, a sort of expectancy, as if they were on the brink of breaking free from the constraints they'd imposed on their relationship.

His phone calls each night had done nothing to disabuse her of this. The timbre of his voice, deep and quiet and intimate, had clothed even as straightforward a question as "How are you, Corinne?" with a subtext that hinted at more than simple concern for her health. If she'd dared, she'd have replied, *Lonely...I miss you...hurry home. Our bed is too empty without you....*

But tonight, she decided, she *would* dare. She'd risk his turning away from her, and tell him everything: about her failed marriage to Joe, but more importantly, about all that lay in her heart now. What could it hurt?

As the afternoon slipped toward dusk, she took a leisurely bath, smoothed scented lotion over her body and put on her favorite maternity gown, the deep purple velvet with the empire waistline. Then, sure the children would be back from their ride by now, she went looking for them.

The house, though, was eerily silent, so much so that the sudden shrill sound of the telephone filled her with an uncanny sense of foreboding as compelling as it was irrational. A stealthy whisper of fear crept up her spine. She knew with prescient certainty that someone dear to her was in serious trouble. She knew it as surely as she knew her own name.

"Raffaello," she breathed, and as if answering, a vicious burst of rain lashed at the windows.

Trembling, she picked up the handset. *"Pronto?"*

"Corinna!"

Relief washed over her at the sound of her mother-in-law's voice. "Malvolia, where are you? It's pouring out."

"Corinna…oh my dear…the children…"

"What about the children?"

"They've disappeared."

God help her, she laughed. "Don't be silly, Malvolia. They can't have."

"They can—they have. We've looked everywhere and there's no sign of them. I'm so afraid they might have wandered away from the estate."

The children are safe as long as they stay on Orsini land….

Corinne's blood turned to ice. Fear stabbed again, sharp as a thousand knives. Her sixth sense had been right on target, except that it wasn't Raffaello in trouble, but the daughter he'd entrusted to her care, and her son, her precious Matthew.

"How long have they been gone?" she asked dully.

"I can't say for sure." Malvolia's voice quivered; verged close to tears. "I wasn't really paying close attention. They were riding in the paddock, just as they always do, and having a good time. Leonora and I went into the stables to shelter from the wind. Suddenly we realized it was too quiet outside, and that's when we discovered…oh, Corinna, what—?"

Hearing the rising hysteria in Malvolia's voice, Corinne stepped in to take control. "Stay put. I'll be right there."

"Please hurry, *cara*."

She severed the connection, grabbed her car keys and within seconds was backing the Cayenne out of the garage and racing along the paved road toward the paddocks at the north perimeter of the estate.

By then, dusk had settled and swathed the land in varying shades of gray, but light shone from the stables, spilling out into the cobblestoned yard where a number of Orsini employees conferred with Malvolia and Leonora.

Dread fused into anger as Corinne braked to a stop next to them. *Why are you standing around talking, instead of searching every nook and cranny for my children?* she wanted to shriek.

But one look at the women's haggard faces, and any censure she might have uttered died on her lips. Guilt and misery etched their features, leaving them looking closer to eighty than sixty. Lowering her window, she said, "It'll be all right. They can't have gone far."

"I'm afraid they might have, *figlia mia*." Malvolia lifted a trembling hand to her mouth. "The ponies are missing, too, you see."

Leonora, normally the one more prone to panic, put a comforting arm around her sister's shoulders. "But already a dozen or more stable and farm hands have started to search, and they know the area very well. I'm sure we'll hear good news soon."

The problem, Corinne thought, scanning the darkening landscape, was that the Orsini lands covered hundreds of acres. The children could be anywhere.

Lorenzo, the head groom, approached the car. "My men will cover every kilometer of land between here and the village, and also along the beach, Signora Orsini. We will find the *bambini* and bring them safely home."

Swallowing the terror clogging her throat, she said, "Do you have any idea which direction they might have taken?"

"We've found an open gate at the end of the lane behind the mobile field shelters. It is likely they went that way and followed one of several paths leading to the village."

He answered with authority, but she picked up on something else; an unspoken hesitation that spelled a different kind of message. "And if they didn't?" she forced herself to ask.

Overhearing, Malvolia shuddered. "There is another path, very steep and rough, heading up into the mountains," she whimpered.

...the land beyond the northern fence is wild and dangerous country....

As clearly as if he stood beside her now, Raffaello's warning came back to haunt Corinne. "I'm checking it out," she said, and ignoring the clamor of objections that arose in response, jammed the Cayenne into gear and roared off.

Ignoring the wide sandy lane beyond the open gate, which she knew led to the shore and from there to the village, she headed the other way, to the north. Searching... searching. Repeating over and over, *Please, God, keep my children safe. Let me find them and bring them home safe again.* And suddenly spying a rutted path on her right. Barely wide enough to accommodate the Cayenne, it snaked up past a grove of ancient olive trees, and without hesitation, she followed it.

Almost immediately, the sandy soil gave way to rough gravel that spat and pinged against the side of the SUV as it jolted and plowed its way uphill. Soon enough, Corinne found herself in inhospitable, isolated territory. The rain had stopped by then, but mist swirled down the mountainside, too thick for her headlights to penetrate more than a few feet ahead.

...wild and dangerous... The words echoed repeatedly through her mind, filling her head with crazy, self-perpetuating fears: of bandits and wild animals poised to strike; of bottomless ravines and rain-flooded creeks that swept away everything lying in their path. And of two little children, lost and cold and afraid, with night closing in. Her beloved Matthew. Raffaello's adored Elisabetta. Lindsay's daughter....

Something scraped the passenger side of the SUV. An outcropping of rock. And looming out of the mist, more of the same. The track had petered out into nothing. She had not found the right path, after all. Worse yet, she was closed in on three sides by towering slabs of rock, in a space so narrow, her only choice was to reverse the SUV until she could turn the vehicle around. No easy task at the best of times. And these were far from that.

The shifting mist deceived her time and again. Loose rocks skidded from beneath her tires and rattled into nothingness. She tried opening her door and leaning out, the better to judge her position on the track, but the bulk of her pregnancy made it impossible. The best she could do was inch along with one foot on the brake.

In the end, her best wasn't good enough. The Cayenne crunched up against something hard, and the next moment tilted at a terrifying angle that left her plastered against the back of her seat. For one endless nanosecond, it rocked gently, hovering between solid ground and heaven only knew what else, its headlights spearing the night in search of the hidden stars. And then it settled precariously, its rear end hanging out in space.

She froze, afraid to move, afraid to breathe.

She and her unborn child were going to die.

She would leave Matthew an orphan, and rob Elisabetta of a mother for the second time.

She would never have the chance to tell Raffaello she loved him.

CHAPTER ELEVEN

LORENZO contacted him when he was one and a half hours out of Milano: Corinne was missing. By some cruel twist of fate, she'd gone looking for the children whom everyone feared were lost, but who'd since been found alive and safe.

Queasy suddenly, Raffaello bellowed, "How the devil could she have just disappeared? Who was the idiot that let her drive off alone? Who left the bloody gate open in the first place?"

But killing the messenger accomplished nothing, and crushing the upsurge of terror churning in his gut, he forced himself into automatic control mode. He knew as well as the next man that in situations like this, a cool head always triumphed over a desperate heart. And he intended to win this latest battle, even if it meant going toe to toe with God Himself.

Ten minutes later, he clicked off the phone and ran a mental check to be sure he'd covered all the bases.

Search party: rounded up.

One Jeep, and one heavy-duty truck equipped with

twelve million candlepower spotlight, towing winch and chains: standing by.

Flashlights, ropes, and two-way radios, emergency foil blankets, medical equipment and supplies: assembled.

By the time the jet landed, everything should be ready to go. Pitifully and agonizingly little though it was, he'd done all a man could do when he found himself captive in an aircraft, cruising at an altitude of twelve thousand meters and a speed in excess of eight hundred kilometers an hour, while all hell broke loose on his home turf.

What he couldn't do was turn back the clock and prevent the crisis from having taken place to begin with. No matter which way he looked at it, his wife was missing, and no amount of cursing or barking orders over the telephone changed that.

Being powerless did not sit well with him. Only once had he found himself its prisoner, and that was when he'd had to watch Lindsay die. He would not let himself be robbed that way again. He would not, *could not* lose Corinne.

He could, he admitted, use a drink; a hefty measure of single malt scotch. But he'd never been one to turn to alcohol when the going got tough, and if ever there was a time that he needed his wits sharp and his head clear, it was now. So he dismissed his steward and, resigning himself to remaining inactive at least for the present, stared out the window. Not that there was anything to see apart from the flashing red light at the tip of the port wing, but that was better than the images waiting to pounce if he dared close his eyes.

They pounced anyway, a bittersweet montage of memories flitting across the black sky in brilliant Technicolor.

The first time he'd seen Corinne, slender as a reed in her

classic black dinner dress and pearls, her eyes as blue as Sicily's summer skies, her hair pale as wheat. He'd noticed she had great legs, a tiny waist, full, firm breasts. And a face that would make any man stop and take a second look. Creamy skin, sweetly curved mouth, delicate cheekbones.

Only as the evening progressed had he taken stock of her other qualities. The pride that wouldn't let her admit she barely made ends meet. Her independent spirit. The stubborn streak a mile wide that had made him want to shake her for refusing to consider his proposal. Even then, instinct had warned him that letting her goad him into rash action would prove a costly mistake that had nothing to do with money. Yet before the evening was over, he'd offered to keep her bed warm, if that's what it would take to seal the deal.

A lousy idea, she'd informed him which, along with her earlier assertion that he was *a few bricks short of a full load* made him smile even at a time such as this. In retrospect, she'd been right. He'd been so sure his heart was safe. There'd been no thunderclap of awareness, no heavenly chorus, none of the dizzy euphoria that had afflicted him the first time he'd set eyes on Lindsay. Corinne's was a more subtle assault, one that infiltrated his complacence when he wasn't looking, and blew it to smithereens.

He'd fallen in love with her in increments. Because she was kind and compassionate and patient. Because she was sensitive to his mother's insecurity, and didn't try to usurp her matriarchal role within the family hierarchy.

Because she didn't force herself on Elisabetta, but waited for the child to come to her. Because she was fair in her dealings with both children, never favoring her own at the expense of his. Because she was never too tired to listen to them, to play with them.

She didn't know how often he'd watched at a distance as she chased them over the lawns, her hair blowing in the breeze, her laughter music to his ears. Or how many times he'd stood at the top of the cliff and spied on her as she played lifeguard, standing waist-deep in the sea as they practiced their swimming. She had no idea how often he lingered outside the nursery, listening as she told Elisabetta about her birth mother; lovely, warm, generous stories full of love and laughter that would keep Lindsay alive forever in her daughter's heart.

Only once had she caught his covert scrutiny, and that had been at dinner, a scant week ago. Even in advanced pregnancy, she was elegant, beautiful, her radiant skin untouched by the harsh Sicilian sun, her profile pure as a cameo, her hair a thick, shining fall of pure pale gold. But seeing him watching her, she'd glanced aside, keeping her thoughts, her inner self, secret from him, and he'd wondered if there'd ever come a time that they'd trust one another enough to share all that lay in their hearts.

He'd wanted to tell her he loved her because she was sexy and desirable. Because she was his, and being around her day-to-day brought him happiness in ways he'd never thought to know again. Because she dared to challenge his pathetic charade of indifference, and forced him to acknowledge his caveman behavior on their so-called honeymoon had been driven by jealousy.

Ever since that time, he'd been so hungry for her, it shamed him. Sleeping in the same bed for the last four months had been nothing short of sublime torture. He'd ached to put his mouth on her belly and kiss their baby through her skin. To touch her in places he knew would leave her sweet and hot and eager for him.

He'd taken enough cold showers to fill an ocean, all to no effect. He wanted her all the time. *All the time.* Wanted to breathe in the fragrance of her skin, and feel her climax when he was gloved deep inside her. And was so deathly afraid he might hurt her or the baby if he gave in to passion raging within him, that he schooled himself to a restraint that nearly killed him.

He didn't know how to kiss her or touch her, and let that be enough. And so he turned away from her, when what he most wanted in the world was to hold her so close that he could feel their baby stirring against *his* belly.

He lay awake for hours, wrestling with his unflagging desire. When fatigue finally claimed him and he fell asleep, he embarrassed himself with dreams he thought he'd outgrown when he was a teenager.

The regrets, the guilt, swamped him. Once, he'd said he had no secrets, that if there was something about him she wanted to know, she only had to ask. But he'd lied. He'd kept his love secret, always waiting for another, better time to share it.

What if he'd left it too late?

The pilot's voice came over the intercom, announcing their final approach to the airfield. Glancing down, Raffaello caught sight of the intermittent flash from the lighthouse on the point ten kilometers east of the village, and moments later, the line of lights marking the runway.

Adrenaline surged through his blood, powerful, stimulating. *Now,* he could wrestle fate to its knees if he had to, instead of hanging fire and depending on blind luck to guide him. He knew better than most that bad things could happen to good people. Look at Lindsay, whose life had been over at twenty-four. But he would not let the same happen to Corinne. Death would not cheat him a second time.

Wherever you are, my love, I will find you and bring you home, he vowed.

The jet touched down and screamed to a stop. At once, he was through the exit door and racing across the tarmac to where one of the Range Rovers idled, with Lorenzo at the wheel. Lorenzo, his head groom, his friend since childhood, and the man he trusted most in the world to cover his back, no matter what.

"Anything new?" he asked, hurling himself into the passenger seat.

Before he had the door closed, the vehicle was in motion, racing through the night to the stables. "Not yet," Lorenzo said.

"No signal from her phone?"

"She didn't take it with her. Your mother found it at the house."

"*Porca miseria!* How often have I told her…!"

"Calm yourself, *mio fratello.* One search party is already out looking for her. The other is ready to go when we join them. We will find her. She'll be home soon."

"She should be home now."

"At least the children are safe."

"For the present," he growled, through clenched teeth. "They might not see it that way when I'm finished with them. What the hell did they think they were doing, taking off like that?"

"They are children, Raffaello, and children don't always think. We both know that."

He scowled. "They will from now on. I'll see to it."

When they arrived in the stable yard, one look at the faces of the men waiting there told him all he needed to know, but he asked anyway. "What's the word from those who went ahead?"

"They've reached the high pastures, *signor,* but so far have found nothing."

Impotent rage rose up and almost choked him. "Then the damn fools have missed something!"

"These are your men, Raffaello," Lorenzo reminded him softly. "They would lay down their lives for you. If they haven't found her, it's not from want of trying, but in weather like this, they could easily miss her."

"Either that, or they're looking in the wrong place. You're sure she headed up the mountain?"

"She said as much."

"She's never had reason to go that way before. I wonder…" He chewed his lip, reconstructing the lay of the land in his mind's eye. Treacherous territory, even for those most familiar with it. For a woman unused to such terrain…

Dio, he couldn't think about that. He dared not. Better to refocus on the idea surfing the corners of his mind. "Remember the time we ran away, Lorenzo, and when we couldn't be found, everyone thought we must be at least halfway to Palermo?"

"And all the time, we were no more than five or six kilometers from home."

"Staked out in a cave at the head of a canyon only you and I knew about."

Lorenzo's gaze locked with his in sudden dread. "Surely you don't think…?"

"At this point, we can't afford to overlook any possibility."

Calling to the waiting men, he outlined the change in plan. No point in going over territory already covered. They would strike out in a new direction.

Within minutes, they were off, four to a vehicle, and followed the trail heading north to the mountains. About five kilometers along, they stopped, and with the aid of flashlights found the clue the first searchers had not thought to look for: tire tracks in the muddy ground, at the point where a rough goat track forked away from the main path.

"God help her, she did go this way," Lorenzo muttered.

The convoy set off again, Raffaello in the lead, following the route she'd taken and inching along at no more than ten kilometers an hour, with all but the drivers playing the beams of the flashlights to either side.

Night and mist turned the landscape into an alien place, one made up of shifting shadows that briefly raised hopes too soon dashed into disappointment.

To one side, the cliff rose steeply. To the other, it dropped thousands of meters to the valley floor. And in between, a track barely wide enough for two cars to pass, paved with loose, uneven rocks, some the size of watermelons. When the branch of a stunted shrub clinging to the upper slope scraped harshly against the side of the Range Rover, Lorenzo voiced what Raffaello had known for some time. "We've made it about as far as we can in these vehicles."

"Then we'll go the rest of the way on foot. Radio the others and tell them we're turning around while we still can."

No mean feat that, but with flashlights signaling the way

and shouted instructions from the rest of the team, the drivers managed, beginning with the heavy truck now leading the pack, and the Range Rover bringing up the rear.

Raffaello's primary concern during this delicate maneuver was safety. He knew well enough that one false move could cost him his life. So when a faint beam of light caught his eye, a few meters farther up the track, he paid little attention, assuming it was a trick of the mist throwing back at him the reflection of his own headlamps as they sliced slowly through the dark. Only after he'd completed the turn and glanced through his rearview mirror did he notice that other pale glow still hanging in the fog-shrouded night. And only then did he understand its significance.

The others had seen it, and they, too, understood. Without needing to be told, they began attaching chains to the truck's tow bar, throwing coiled ropes over their shoulders, debating the best course of action.

Raffaello didn't wait to find out what that might be. All he knew, all that mattered was ascertaining if they'd found Corinne's car and if she was still inside it, alive and unhurt.

Cursing his leather-soled loafers, which were never designed for mountain climbing, he slipped and slid his way over the scree until he reached the source of that painfully weak gleam of light. Then, he froze in his tracks, transfixed by the sight in front of him.

His heart almost seized up. The Cayenne sat perilously balanced on a slab of rock at a bend in the path, its back wheels suspended in space. Even as he broke out in a cold sweat of horror, the body of the car rocked slightly, like the pendulum of a stopped clock about to start marking time again.

Lorenzo, following close behind him, skidded to a halt. *"Dio santo!"* he whispered. "Is she in there?"

"I can't tell from here," he said, and started to edge forward, one careful step at a time.

But Lorenzo caught him by the arm and held him back. "Wait," he cautioned. "There are others here, better able than either of us, to deal with this."

"This," he ground out, the metallic taste of fear thick on his tongue, "happens to be my wife. Do not ask me to wait."

"And if, in your haste, you send her to her death, how will you live with yourself, Raffaello?" his friend inquired. "Step away, for the love of God, and let those who know how, do what has to be done."

The fight went out of him and numb with despair, he nodded. He'd once hauled an overturned tractor upright; carried an injured man half his weight again to a first-aid station on Etna. But not even his mighty strength was enough to lift the Cayenne to safety. For once, he had to stand back and rely on the expertise of others.

Two wiry mechanics who looked after his farm equipment—husbands and fathers just like him with every bit as much to lose as he had—conferred briefly, clipped themselves to safety lines strung from the Jeep, and approached the SUV, moving as lightly, as carefully, as if they stepped on eggs. One aimed a flashlight while the other took the end of the heavy chain attached to the truck and hooked it to the Cayenne's frame.

Raffaello's blood froze as the car shuddered and rocked wildly. Then, the most beautiful sound in the world rumbled through the canyon—that of the powerful electric winch grinding into action and hauling its precious cargo to safety. The chain grew tight. Slowly, one agonizing centimeter at a time and screaming objections at the damage to its undercarriage, the Cayenne tipped away from danger and toward solid ground.

A cheer went up, and died quickly as the truck spotlight settled on the other vehicle's windshield and pinpointed the unmoving figure in the driver's seat. For a moment, Raffaello stood rooted to the spot, afraid of what he was about to learn; afraid not to know. Then tearing free of Lorenzo's restraining hands, he rushed forward and wrenched open the door.

She leaned against the headrest, the seat belt tight across her hips but hidden by the bulk of her pregnancy. She looked pale as moonlight, was cold when he touched her at the corner of her jaw, but her pulse was strong, and when he laid his hand on her belly, he felt their baby playing football inside.

"Corinne, *dolce amore*," he breathed, bending over her and stroking her beautiful face.

He knew all about hell, but had never really believed in heaven until that moment, when she opened her eyes and said drowsily, "Before I die, there's something I must tell you. I love you, Raffaello."

"You're not going to die," he murmured thickly. "I won't let you. I'm taking you home and never letting you out of my sight again."

She blinked and almost smiled, then reared up in the seat and clutched frantically at his hands. "Oh, Raffaello, the children—!"

"Are safe," he soothed her. "Their ponies showed more sense than they did and brought them back where they belong."

"How...?"

"The hows and whys can wait. Right now, we need to get you out of here." Carefully he unbuckled her seat belt and eased her out of the car. "Does anything hurt, *tesoro?*"

"My legs," she said, slumping against him. "They've gone to sleep."

Overhearing, Lorenzo asked, "Do you need the stretcher?"

Raffaello lifted her into his arms. "No," he said, sounding more like himself, and another cheer, more sustained this time, went up from the waiting group. Someone came forward to wrap a blanket around her shoulders, someone else spread another over the backseat of the Range Rover.

He climbed in beside her, and rested her head in his lap. She was shivering, from shock probably, but Lorenzo was already behind the wheel, with the engine running and the heater blasting. "Straight to the villa?" he asked, over his shoulder. "Or should I head for the nearest hospital?"

"The hospital," Raffaello said.

"No," she said. "Home."

"You should be checked over by a doctor, just to be sure, *amore mio.*"

"I don't need a doctor, I need you." She sighed and reached for his hand. "There's so much I have to say, Raffaello—things I should have told you a long time ago."

"And I you," he said. "I could spend a month cataloging my failures and shortcomings as a husband, but at this moment, the only words that really matter are that I love you."

In some ways, their return reminded her of the first time she'd set foot in the villa's grand entrance hall. But she saw it all now with a fresh eye; with an appreciation less for its elegant frescoed ceilings and wonderful arched windows, and more for the people waiting to greet her. The household staff, their smiles warmer than anything a blanket could offer. The children, so angelic in their pajamas it was hard to believe them capable of mischief. And Malvolia and Leonora, their poor faces drawn with anxiety and remorse.

"Ah, *figlia mia.*" Her mother-in-law wept, folding Corinne in a hug and pressing kisses to her cheeks, "can you ever forgive me?"

Not to be outdone, Leonora shoehorned her way into the embrace. "Please believe that we would never deliberately hurt the children, Corinna."

"Of course I believe you," she said, hugging them back. "I know how much you love them."

"And you, *carissima!*" Malvolia cried. "You are my daughter, my child. I was so afraid I would never see you again. What can I do to prove it to you?"

"I'd love to soak in a hot bath and change into something comfortable," she said, hoping to avoid a sobfest of mammoth proportions. "Then, you could feed me, if you like. I'm starving."

The words were scarcely out of her mouth before the staff jumped into action, Gastone sending a maid scurrying upstairs to fill the tub, and Filomena herding her crew back to the kitchen.

"But first," Corinne amended, when it was just the six of them left in the hall, "I'd like to give my children a big kiss." She held out her arms. "Come here, you little monkeys, and tell me what happened this afternoon, that you put the entire household into such an uproar."

Matthew raced over and barreled into her so hard, she'd have toppled over if Raffaello hadn't kept a firm grip on her. "Poopy pony ran away," he said indignantly. "He's a bad boy."

But Elisabetta hung back, her lower lip trembling.

"Come here, honey," Corinne said gently, disentangling herself from her son who showed not the slightest remorse for his shenanigans. "Right now, I could really use a hug from my girl, as well."

At that, Elisabetta flew to her and buried her face against her swollen belly. "It was my fault, Mommy," she wailed. "I shouldn't have let us go. Now you won't love me anymore."

So much for avoiding a sobfest! Corinne had held it together pretty well until that point, too glad and relieved that everyone was safe, to dwell on how close they'd come to tragedy. But Elisabetta broke her heart with that telling remark.

Tears rolling down her face, she lowered herself to her knees and held the little thing close. "I'll never not love you, darling," she whispered, when she could catch her breath enough to be coherent. "You're my special girl, and nothing will ever change that."

"I'm not as inclined to be forgiving," Raffaello said sternly, helping her to feet. "You two haven't heard the last of this. Go to the nursery and wait there for me."

"Don't be so hard on them," Corinne begged, watching as they made their doleful way upstairs. "They've been through enough for one day."

"What about what they've put the rest of us through?"

"They made a mistake."

"They put you and our baby in danger."

"And you rescued us." She leaned into him, loving the solid feel of his body, the strength of his arm around her. "A happy ending, for a change, Raffaello. Let's not spoil it."

Tightening his hold, he guided her up the stairs. "Not an ending, but a beginning, *amore mio,*" he replied, the look in his eye making her blush. "And it's about to start now."

CHAPTER TWELVE

FIRST, THEY STOPPED BY the nursery. "Because," Corinne pointed out, when he would have made straight for the master suite, "it's unfair to send them to bed without letting them know they're forgiven."

"Forgiven, my left foot!" he retorted. "Elisabetta was right. She knew better than to leave the property. *Dio,* Corinne, it's not as if they don't have space enough here to roam around pretty much wherever they like."

"You're forgetting she didn't act alone. You heard Matthew. The little imp probably goaded her into breaking the rules."

"If he did, he came by it honestly. You do a pretty good job yourself of making a person forget the rules, and here's the proof of that." He stroked her belly, the tenderness in his voice putting paid to his annoyance.

"Some rules are meant to be broken."

Sobering again, he said, "Not by our children, my darling. At least, not until they're old enough to understand the consequences. You could have died this afternoon, and while I won't overemphasize that with them because I think they're already frightened enough by what they did,

I do intend to make it very clear I won't tolerate such behavior again. Are we together on this, Corinne, or do I go
in there and deal with them by myself?"

"We're together," she said, slipping her arm through
his. "Always and forever."

She thought she knew what intimacy was all about, but that
evening, he brought new and deeper meaning to the word,
one that combined tenderness with passion, and murmured
words of love that broke down all the barriers she'd thrown
up in her misguided attempts to remain heart-whole.

"Now that that's over with, I have a confession to make,"
she began, the minute they'd put their chastened children
to bed and were alone in their own suite, supposedly
dressing for dinner.

"Shut up, *angelo mio,*" he said softly. "I have waited
long enough to do this and won't be put off a minute longer." And to make sure she fell in with his wishes, he
captured her mouth with his.

If all he ever did was kiss her, she would be a happy
woman, she thought dizzily, surrendering herself to him.
But he had more in mind and murmuring to her between
kisses, he deftly stripped away her clothes until she stood
before him as she never had before, with lamplight illumi-
nating every lush curve and contour. Self-conscious suddenly, she tried to cover herself—an exercise in futility,
considering how much of her there was—but he impris-
oned her hands in one of his, and skimmed his other over
her breasts and belly to her thighs, all the time subjecting
her to a slow, unblinking inspection that left her skin puck-
ering with heated delight.

She knew then that kisses would never be enough. Every part of her, every pore, every strand of hair, needed him as a flower needed water.

"*Sei bella,*" he whispered. "You are beautiful, my Corinne."

"I'm huge," she said.

He shook his head, his eyes scouring the length of her a second time. "You are a goddess."

"Who's sort of lied to you about her past."

"You served time behind bars?" he inquired, lazily cupping one full breast in his palm.

A shiver of pure pleasure raced up her spine. "Nothing that extreme," she said breathlessly. "Just something I should have told you a long time ago."

He steered her into the bathroom and handed her into the sunken tub, which the maid had prepared. "Then whatever it is can wait a few minutes longer."

Wreathed in scented coils of steam, she watched, heavy-eyed, as he tossed aside his own clothes and joined her, sliding in behind her and pulling her against him so that her spine rested against his chest and the water lapped at her chin. "*Va bene,*" he said, the words grazing her ear like a caress, "I'm listening."

Now that the moment was finally at hand, all the reasonable explanations she'd rehearsed slipped from her mind. "I wasn't happily married to Joe," she said baldly. "In fact, I was almost relieved when it came to an end. Not that I was glad he died, you understand—he was much too young for that—but because I didn't have to keep trying to fix what I knew had been broken almost from the beginning."

"I see," he said. "And you couldn't tell me this before, because…?"

"I was jealous. You and Lindsay got it right the first time, and were so happy together. Just from the way you spoke, I knew that you had such reverence for marriage, and I was afraid if you knew about mine, you'd think less of me for not trying harder to make it work."

"You worried for nothing, *tesoro*. I'd never hold myself up as an expert on making a marriage work. I might have got it right, as you put it, with Lindsay, but look how close I've come to ruining ours because I was too blind to recognize a gem when one landed in my lap."

"You don't have to say that, Raffaello. I knew from the outset that you didn't marry me for love."

"No," he said, "I didn't. With you, the order was reversed. I married you first, then I fell in love with you. But Corinne, *angelo mio, anima mia,* that doesn't mean I love you less."

He rested his chin on her head and was silent a moment. When he spoke again, his voice trembled. "This afternoon, when I thought I might have lost you, I didn't know how I'd go on. Were it not for the children, I'm not sure I'd have wanted to. But you're here now, and I thank God for giving me a second chance to show you how much you mean to me."

Turning her head, she kissed his jaw. "You are my life, Raffaello. I am so honored to be your wife, so proud to be carrying your child."

"I would take you to bed now, if I could," he murmured. His flesh stirring urgently against the small of her back, "but I know my mother still hasn't forgiven herself for causing us so much distress, and if we don't put in an appearance for dinner, she'll worry all night long that we haven't forgiven her, either. But later, my love…"

"Later," she echoed, a thrill of anticipation streaming through her blood.

But later came sooner than either of them anticipated. Drying each other metamorphosed into an exploration that went far beyond the mundane, and somehow they were on the bed and he was kissing her all over and she was reaching for him and whimpering with need.

He took her breath away. She had never felt more loved. The entire universe narrowed until there was nothing but the feel of his skin against hers, the taste and scent of him filling her senses. And finally, the fierce strength of him inside her, smooth as marble, hot as fire.

"It is not safe," he muttered hoarsely, desperately trying to stem the passion coursing between them.

But safety was all about lying in his arms, with him buried so deeply inside her that they were as one. Safety came from hearing him say *I love you,* and for her daring to say, *I love you, too.* Safety was knowing that her heart had found a home at last.

Touching her finger to her tongue, she dipped it in the hollow of his throat. "I'm branding you," she whispered, echoes of passion lingering in her voice. "Now you're mine."

"I've been yours almost from the day I first saw you," he said. "I just didn't know it at the time."

Later, after they were dressed finally, she lifted her hair so that he could fasten her pearls around her neck. "This is the last time you wear these," he grumbled, struggling with the clasp. "I shall buy you the finest to be found, one for every second of happiness you have brought me, and all strung together with a diamond clasp that works as it should."

"I don't need diamonds or pearls," she said. "I have you and our children. Which reminds me. If the baby's a girl, I think we should call her Lindsay."

But he shook his head. "No, *amore mio*. This is our child. Yours and mine. I loved Lindsay, but I came to terms with her death before I even knew you. She is part of my past and I'll never forget her, but the future belongs to you and me."

His mother and aunt seemed to be of the same opinion, albeit for different reasons. "We have reached a decision," Malvolia announced over a fabulous dinner of crayfish bisque and poached fish. "You have been very tolerant of our meddling, Corinna, but you are the mistress of this house now, and it's time my sister and I moved to the dowager villa."

Once upon a time, she'd have welcomed such news, but that was before when her insecurity had left her vulnerable to the slightest hint of criticism. "I won't hear of it," she said. "You belong here. I need you, this baby needs you, and so do your other grandchildren."

"You're a sweet girl to say so," Malvolia said, sudden tears sparkling in her dark eyes, "but I think we proved today that we are not nearly as necessary to your happiness as we liked to think and are, in fact, more of a liability than an asset."

"Tell them they're wrong," Corinne said, appealing to Raffaello.

He shrugged. "They are wrong only if you say so, *tesoro*. Because my mother is right. You are the mistress of this house and you decide whom you want living under its roof."

"I want you," she said, encompassing both women in a steady gaze. "More than that, I need you. You've taught me what real family is all about and that's something I never knew until I came here. Please don't take it away from me now. And please don't cry," she added, as Leonora buried her face in her napkin and gave way to an emotional outburst of weeping. "This is a happy day, a wonderful day. We are all here, safe and well, with enough love to go around for everyone to get his and her fair share. So let there be no more talk of anyone moving out. We are a family and we belong together."

"You are right about one thing," Malvolia said, succumbing to tears herself. "There is more love here than I have known in years. I see it when my son looks at you, Corinna, and when you look at him. I hear it when you take my grandson on your lap and sing to him, when you fill my granddaughter's heart with stories of her birth mother. And I hope you feel it when my sister and I look at you because, *figlia mia,* you have become so very, very dear to our hearts."

Either the crying was contagious or her hormones were in more of an uproar than usual. "Well, it's settled, then," she said, surreptitiously wiping away a tear.

"I hope so, because Filomena has made cannoli, your favorite dessert, my darling, and it would be a crime to ruin it by drowning it," Raffaello said, raising his wineglass. "So let me propose a toast. To my wife, who has brought more joy to all our lives than any of us ever hoped for or had the right to expect."

Ten days later, Corinne went into labor, and as it turned out, the question of choosing a girl's name didn't arise because, early on the morning of December 15, she gave birth to a nine pound, four ounce boy.

Raffaello was at her side from the first, doing all the things that strong men do when they watch their wives struggle to bring a new life into the world. He wiped the sweat from her brow, spurred her on to fresh effort when exhaustion sapped her strength and uttered not a word of complaint when she gripped his hand so tightly that she almost crushed the bones in his fingers.

He told her she was brave and wonderful and beautiful. He turned pale when the baby's head presented, and cried unashamedly when their son made his lusty debut.

"He's perfect," she said, when he placed the baby in her arms.

"*Si*," Raffaello whispered, showering her face with featherlight kisses. "Just like his mother."

She brought her new son home from the hospital that same evening, to find the house dressed up for Christmas, with twinkling lights and trees in every room, carols playing softly on the stereo, gifts for the baby piled high in the nursery and a huge bouquet of gorgeous red roses in the bedroom.

"A dozen for each child," Raffaello told her, when all the excitement had died down and they were at last alone in bed together. Then taking a black velvet box hidden among the blooms' soft, fragrant petals, he withdrew an engagement ring, a magnificent diamond solitaire.

"As usual, I'm doing things in reverse order," he said, sliding it next to the wedding band on the third finger of her left hand, "but even though it comes almost a year after I asked you to marry me, know that, just like my love for you, I give it to you now because a diamond is forever."

"I like that word, 'forever,'" she said, sinking into the warmth of his embrace.

"Why is that, *adorata?*"

"Because all my life I've searched and at last, here on your wild and beautiful island, my heart has found its home. With you. Forever."

researching the cure

The facts you need to know:

- Breast cancer is the most common form of cancer in the United Kingdom. **One woman in nine** will be affected by the disease in her lifetime.

- Every year over **44,000** women, **300** men are diagnosed with breast cancer and around **12,500** women and approximately **100** men will die from the disease.

- 80% of all breast cancers occur in post-menopausal women and approximately 8,800 pre-menopausal women are diagnosed with the disease each year.

- However, the five year survival rate has significantly improved, on average today 80% of women diagnosed with the disease will still be alive five years later, compared to 52% thirty years ago.

Breast Cancer Campaign's mission is to beat breast cancer by funding innovative world-class research to understand how breast cancer develops, leading to improved diagnosis, treatment, prevention and cure.

4 FREE

BOOKS AND A SURPRISE GIFT!

We would like to take this opportunity to thank you for reading this Mills & Boon® book by offering you the chance to take FOUR more specially selected titles from the Modern™ series absolutely FREE! We're also making this offer to introduce you to the benefits of the Mills & Boon® Book Club—

- ★ **FREE home delivery**
- ★ **FREE gifts and competitions**
- ★ **FREE monthly Newsletter**
- ★ **Exclusive Mills & Boon® Book Club offers**
- ★ **Books available before they're in the shops**

Accepting these FREE books and gift places you under no obligation to buy, you may cancel at any time, even after receiving your free shipment. Simply complete your details below and return the entire page to the address below. You don't even need a stamp!

YES! Please send me 4 free Modern books and a surprise gift. I understand that unless you hear from me, I will receive 6 superb new titles every month for just £2.99 each, postage and packing free. I am under no obligation to purchase any books and may cancel my subscription at any time. The free books and gift will be mine to keep in any case.

P8ZED

Ms/Mrs/Miss/Mr ....Initials ....

BLOCK CAPITALS PLEASE

Surname ....

Address ....

....

....Postcode...............................

Send this whole page to:
UK: FREEPOST CN81, Croydon, CR9 3WZ